KING PENGUIN

## A KINDNESS CUP

Born in Brisbane, Thea Astley studied at the University of Queensland. She has published ten novels and one collection of short stories. Three of her novels have won Australia's prestigious Miles Franklin Award: *The Well-Dressed Explorer* (1962), *The Slow Native* (1965), and *The Acolyte* (1972). In 1975 her novel *A Kindness Cup* won the Australian Book of the Year Award. *Hunting the Wild Pineapple*, a collection of short stories, won the James Cook Foundation of Australian Literature Studies Award in 1980.

Thea Astley recently retired from the position of Fellow in Australian Literature at Macquarie University and is now living and writing full time in New South Wales, Australia.

*Beachmasters, Girl with a Monkey, An Item from the Late News, The Well-Dressed Explorer,* and *It's Raining in Mango* are all available from Penguin.

# A
# KINDNESS
# CUP

*by*

*Thea Astley*

A KING PENGUIN
PUBLISHED BY PENGUIN BOOKS

PENGUIN BOOKS
Published by the Penguin Group
Viking Penguin, a division of Penguin Books USA Inc.,
40 West 23rd Street, New York, New York 10010, U.S.A.
Penguin Books Ltd, 27 Wrights Lane,
London W8 5TZ, England
Penguin Books Australia Ltd, Ringwood,
Victoria, Australia
Penguin Books Canada Ltd, 2801 John Street,
Markham, Ontario, Canada L3R 1B4
Penguin Books (N.Z.) Ltd, 182–190 Wairau Road,
Auckland 10, New Zealand

Penguin Books Ltd, Registered Offices:
Harmondsworth, Middlesex, England

First published in Australia by
Thomas Nelson (Australia) Ltd. 1974
First published in the United States of America
in one volume with *The Acolyte* under the
title *Two by Astley* by G. P. Putnam's Sons 1988
Published in Penguin Books 1989

1  3  5  7  9  10  8  6  4  2

Copyright © Thea Astley, 1974
All rights reserved

LIBRARY OF CONGRESS CATALOGING IN PUBLICATION DATA
Astley, Thea.
A kindness cup/ by Thea Astley.
p.   cm. — (A King Penguin)
ISBN 0 14 01.1780 6
I. Title.
[PR9619.3.A75K5   1989]
823—dc19      89–30035

Printed in the United States of America
Set in Galliard

Except in the United States of America, this
book is sold subject to the condition that it
shall not, by way of trade or otherwise, be lent,
re-sold, hired out, or otherwise circulated
without the publisher's prior consent in any form
of binding or cover other than that in which it
is published and without a similar condition
including this condition being imposed on the
subsequent purchaser.

*Should auld acquaintance be forgot*
  *And never brought to min'?*
*Should auld acquaintance be forgot*
  *And days o' lang syne?*
*For auld lang syne, my dear,*
  *For auld lang syne,*
*We'll tak' a cup o' kindness yet,*
  *For auld lang syne.*

—ROBERT BURNS

## ACKNOWLEDGMENTS

The impetus for this novel came from an actual incident at The Leap, Queensland, in the second half of the last century; but this cautionary fable makes no claim to being a historical work. Liberties have been taken with places and times, and the author happily admits possible anachronisms.

Acknowledgments are made to the report of the Select Committee on the Native Police Force, Queensland, 1861.

THIS WORLD is the unreality, he thinks between smiles and frowns over the letter.

After twenty years—back!

They'd done it after ten—a folly he'd ignored. Back to The Taws. After all these longitudes of time, what would that make them all if all of them could make it? Trembling sexagenarians, hearts pausing— but not for joy; eyes cataracted, prostates swollen or excised, livers cirrhosed, hearing dimmed.

This man pauses in his shaving to squint at the piece of paper again, razor hesitant, eye returning anxious but reluctant to the blurred letters. Who is Barney Sweetman? A name he has tried to forget. Barney . . . Sweetman? Jesus! Sweetman Sweetman Sweetman? Raintrees outside the stock-and-station agent's before the dogmatic through road eased round by the school. Where he. Under crushing dust. Velvet crushes. And the flies busy. A youngish man then. And that other youngish as well, weighing out some sort of glittering utterance with his face ju-jubed by School of Arts stained glass, frecklings of cerulean and jonquil in lamp-light. From shadow into heat and buggies, dozy cobs blinkered in shafts by a water-trough. The slipperiest of memories. Had that been Barney Sweetman, later town councillor, mayor, State member, mutton-chopped hearty? Retired now? Conniving now?

He nicks himself and the tired blood trickles a moment, stops easily these days almost before the cotton-wool sticks.

Crumples the letter that morning. Picks it out of the bin that night, hearing wind along the Moreton Bay reaches moving out of the sea into the empty passageways of his house with its too many lumps of darkening furniture and the whisky bottle too handy. Smooths it out again and licks at the strange invitation a little, the liquor moist on his lip. The impersonal jargon of some bleeding go-getter, he tells himself, making a quick quid on the boosted tourist tears of returning townsfolk! Why, his bay is filled with tears and the figs of its name, the long roots stretching, groping down in laterals to weep over slight grey waters with islands humped and sand-duned and afloat. He is drenched in nostalgia here. What is the point, any point, in a return?

My filled days, he thinks ironically, my filled days. With walks along the front, a shambles to the pier and along it to the point where winds knot green swirl of sea and gull and fish and some crumbling other man casting his lines. Back to the figged park and the bottle-lollied picnic kiosk, and an hour or so beneath broad leaves pecking at book or paper. Barney Sweetman. The bastard, he says. And Buckmaster. Buckmaster and Sweetman. Knighted for milking God's earth. Knighted for handling the sugar strikes. Knighted for owning more acres of sweet grass in the north than any man had the right to control. But not knighted for that noon at Mandarana—how the names come back now!—the virtue guards with rifles kicking their unwilling horses up the runty slopes while the natives scuttled like roos from bush to bush until the high plateau. Or after. The down-curve through hot air and the body whizzing.

He closes his eyes.


"Boys," Mr Dorahy said, "let us recapitulate . . .

"I cannot believe," he continued musingly, his finger poised at a certain section of the Gallic Wars, "that men are rational beings when I observe their militaristic antics. I mean the drill protocol claptrap, of course, quite apart from the specifics of learning how to kill." His thin and rather sour face was extremely gentle. He smiled with the terrible snaggle teeth that all who had grown to love failed now to notice. "What do you think, Jenner?"

"Are you serious, sir?"

"Of course."

"But we have our own sort of drill, sir. I mean terms and classroom behaviour and . . ."

"When," Mr Dorahy interrupted, but still gently, "have I ever required a clicking to, a standing to, a goose-stepping hop to it?"

Jenner's round sixteen-year-old face began a small grin. "We just do it, sir."

"You miss my point, boy. You miss it." Dorahy sighed and stared bleakly past the eight faces to the school paddock, still being fenced, at workmen whacking on wood for the new school block beyond the pepper-trees.

"Close your Livy," he said tiredly. "If you'll give me all that keen attention of yours, I'll try to draw a parallel."

"Parable, sir?" a shaggy lad next to Jenner inquired with a smirk.

"If you like," Mr Dorahy said. He could feel reluctance lumping his tongue. "*If* you like. Tarquinius Sextus, as you will recall, was a bastard par excellence." The boys began to laugh quietly. "His bastardry," continued Mr Dorahy without a muscle-twitch of amusement, "entered the fields of male folly which ruined not only himself, I mean his soul, but a family line!"

He began to quote but no one understood, so he dragged himself from his chair and scribbled the Latin on the board. "Buckmaster," he said, "translate."

The clock hands were staggering. Time passed slowly in that cube of heat and flies. Clause gobbets. Literal patches of historic infinitive. Torture, Dorahy decided. Sheer mindless torture. He said, "Take over, Jenner."

Jenner bumbled for a while, testing words with his incompetent tongue. He crashed over the last sentence—". . . and there to her surprise Tarquinius found her lying unclad."

Dorahy coughed. He coughed out this dust and the dust became the expectations of three failed years.

"A little more delicately, I think: 'And there surprised Lucretia lying naked.' It was Tarquin who did the surprising in the literal sense of the word, boys. Not the unfortunate lady. Though doubtless she, too, was surprised in your sense. I'll read it to you again. 'And there the Tarquin, black and forceful, surprised Lucretia lying naked.' " He repeated the last two words softly and a terrible adolescent excitement charged the room. The angle of his vowel, that first vowel, lecherously over-toned plus the quiet refinement of the soured mouth and face made for frightful antithesis.

Outside a world of trees and umber. Flies inside drumming window-heat, taking glass for air.

13

"The militaristic claptrap and the insolvency of the rapist are equally sub-human—is what I mean. Is very much what I mean."

Buckmaster didn't quite scowl. He was later to sire three half-castes. "Women!" he whispered hissingly along the row. "Gins!" he whispered. And he scrawled furtively a set of parted legs on the margin of his Livy.

"If your thinking, Buckmaster," Mr Dorahy proceeded gently, "lies only in the force of your genitals, God help the world."

Buckmaster senior later said, leaning on his silver-topped riding crop, "You cannot speak to the boys like this. There are certain matters. Things such as . . . Decencies must . . ."

"In this noisome little colony," Mr Dorahy replied mildly with more sweat than usual running down the edges of his weary hair, "where masculinity is top dog, it seems to me that some occasional thought should be given, chivalrously you understand—*do* you understand?—to the sex that endures most of our nastiness."

"You're mad," Buckmaster said.

"You become that which you do."

Mr Buckmaster allowed himself a tiny bleached smile. "Any bloody teacher in this place would have to be mad."

"I meant you," Mr Dorahy said. The small scar of some long-forgotten protest whitened on his cheek. "Would you want your son to become one of the mindless, insensitive, money-grubbing bulls you see around this town and that he gives every indication of aping?"

"I'll have you sacked, by Christ!" Pulling at his crotch. His cutaway donned for the occasion—running the bejesus out of a back-town schoolie—stank in the heat. Summer was crouching all over the town.

"Please do," Mr Dorahy said. "I am so tired."

But it did not could not happen. Who else was there for a pittance in a provisional school slapped hard in the sweating sugar-grass north of the tropic?

I am single, Mr Dorahy told himself proceeding through the drudgeries of instruction. I am single and thirty-seven and in love with landscape. Even this. Other faces cut close to the heart. His assistants, say, who took the junior forms. Married and widowed Mrs Wylie gathering in the chickens for a spot of rote tables or spelling, beating it out in an unfinished shack at the boundary fence. Or Tom Willard with his combined primary forms and his brimstone lay-preaching on

14

the Sabbath. Or himself as a gesture to culture, keeping on the bigger boys of his parish, for he was priestly enough to use that word, for a bit of elementary classics and a purging of Wordsworth. It all seemed useless, as foolish as trying to put Tintern Abbey into iambic hexameters. He had come with a zealot's earnestness, believing a place such as this might need him. And there was, after all, only loneliness; he was cut off from the pulse of the town, although, he insisted to himself rationalising furiously, he had been regularly to meetings of the Separation League and had blown only occasional cold air on their hot. He had drunk with the right men. He had kept his mouth closed. He had assumed nothing. And yet other faces, the wrong sort because they were black, had their own especial tug, the sad black flattened faces of the men working with long knives in the cane and their scabby children making games in the dust at the entrances and exits of towns. The entrances. The exits. Observe that, he cautioned himself.

He was friendly with them, as friendly perhaps as Charlie Lunt on his hopeless block of land west of the township; friendly even when they robbed his accessible larder, noting the small fires they made at the boundary fences of his shack; or when he caught Kowaha, shinily young, pilfering sugar and flour, eyes rolling like humbugs with the lie of it while he did a bishop's candlesticks—"But I gave them to you"—confusing her entirely. Bastardry not intended, he told his ironic self. Yet she asked next time, and the next, always at half-light so that the scurrilous tongues of settlers along the road were never sure of shadow or concretion.

*Nort,* Mr Dorahy inscribed meticulously on Buckmaster's ill-spelled prose. *Nort,* he gently offered, as Trooper Lieutenant Fred Buckmaster gave his evidence before the select committee.

Do you think, the magistrate, a bottle-coloured Irishman, had asked, you should be cognisant of the facts before you take your measures? Have you no written or printed instructions?

No printed ones, Lieutenant Buckmaster said, truculent and oiling slightly. I act on letters received from squatters.

Do you think, the magistrate pursued, hating the stinking obese fellow before him, that it is right to pursue these blacks—say a month after their depredations?

I always act immediately, Lieutenant Buckmaster said flatly, immediately I am called upon. But it is the tribe I follow. Not individuals.

You can never see the actual depredators. (Conjugate that verb, Dorahy whispered to himself. Oh, conjugate it, man!)

Mr Sheridan tapped his fingers on the edge of the greasy desk. He was not in love with his job.

Do you not think there is any other way of dealing with them except by shooting them?

Lieutenant Buckmaster smiled.

No. I don't think they can understand anything else but shooting. At least that is the case as far as my experience goes.

And your experience goes a long way, does it not? Another point, then. Tell me, are your police boys in the habit of taking the gins from the tribes . . . for whatever purpose?

Buckmaster edged slightly. His real rash irritated, but this was now a rash of the mind. It was very hot in the little court.

No. Except with my instructions.

Did they take any this way in the previous case at Kuttabul?

No. Buckmaster could not conceal his contempt. There were no young gins there. Only old ones. Later some young gins followed us up from the Kuttabul scrub.

And do they stay with you? The magistrate could not blur his wonder.

No, Lieutenant Buckmaster admitted. They only stop a night and get a piece of tobacco in the morning and go away. (Mr Sheridan raised his eyebrows at this point.) But generally we have to flog them off. They will follow the men all over the country. I have known them to follow my boys for as long as five days and I have had to flog them off in the middle of the night.

Have you indeed? Mr Sheridan inquired, unable to control himself. And watched with interest the slow red on the lieutenant's ruined face.

Dorahy had been observed by the port-nosed Buckmaster allowing some slight scrap of black flesh to depart his humpy unmolested long after sunset. So long after sunset that Buckmaster was returning from his own bodily revenge on a depressed white woman who ran an out-of-town shanty on the Mandarana road. His sexual angers were unsatisfied, not merely because of the fifth-rate partner who accepted his adulterous attentions like a necessary lash but by sighting a sleek gin slipping with a sugar-bag of something from the sour schoolmaster's. "To be in charge of my boy!" he raved inwardly, kicking his horse into a canter. Its nervous rump responded quiveringly to the crop. He could have been flogging Dorahy or the gin or the woman he had just left.

All around him, however, was the benison of cane arrowing on the back roads to his farm, the beige spearhead of flower proving gentleness. Yet he was sickened by cycles of it and sometimes wondered if he really were committed to farm.

His own house was pocked with slow pools of light from the kerosene lamps along the back veranda where he found, gripping the rage within his flesh, son Fred playing a game of chess with young Jenner.

Both boys stared curiously at this unsated man who communicated distemper with his first words.

"Where's your mother?"

Fred dangled a lost pawn. It was an insolent gesture over-interpreted by the father who saw himself thus. "Sewing," Fred said. "In the front room."

His father could have been choking when he roared, "And what are you two wasting time on now? We don't keep you on at school like bloody gentlemen, you know, simply to fritter. Yes, fritter, by God! This is the last year of it and then you'll have to earn your keep. Slumped around here!" His voice was lumpy with scorn.

"It gives you a certain prestige," Fred said unwisely, "having an unemployed wastrel adult son."

"By the living Christ," Buckmaster roared, "I won't take, I don't have to take *that!*" Slamming his broad hand across the side of his son's thick head.

Young Jenner said, offering his handkerchief towards the bloody nose, "It's true, you know. My father reckons we'll do much better for ourselves. Ever so much better."

"With your piddling bits of filthy Latin! With your sexless poets, your witless grammarians!"

(He has quite a flow, Jenner commented later to Fred, for an uneducated man.) Now he said, "We can't help it, sir. We're the victims of parenthood."

Mr Buckmaster had moved to the wine-rack near the kitchen door.

17

"I am an important man in this town," he stated redundantly. "I have thirty boys working for me on the farm. I must have a son who can control, share with me, know how to handle men."

Young Buckmaster was too absorbed in blood and shame to dribble anything but snivels into this.

"Your father," Buckmaster pressed on, gulping some ferocious indigo liquid that always failed to make him feel better, and swinging on young Jenner, "is a step beyond my reasoning. The biggest property in the district. Two score of Kanaks hauling in his profits. What does it matter what his soft-haired boy does, eh? What the hell does it matter? You'll sleep sweet on a sugar-bed as long as you live and you can take this fancy education from that snot-nosed teacher of yours and whatever it does for you, for it won't do much but make you useless when it comes to dealing with men!" (He was fond of dealing with men, was Buckmaster, and could handle women in much the same way.) "So I'd thank you to keep your privileged presence and fancy ideas"—the chessboard was scattered at this point across the veranda flooring—"to yourself."

In protest Jenner cried out, "But it was for Mrs Buckmaster I called. My mother sent over a book she had asked for."

Mr Buckmaster, slowed by wine, thought this one over.

"Sewing, you said?" His son nodded sullenly. "Not reading? Not wasting the light?" He mumbled into his glass some winey incantations and, as on cue, his wife came through suddenly from the front of the house to ignore her son's bloodied face and begin stoking up the last of the fire to make tea. She was forty and ruined, not so much by her husband as by the country and the tyranny of it.

A strange woman, the neighbours said, and would continue to say for her resistance both to them and to her husband who had used her as an incubator to breed sons but extracted only daughters except for this youngest, gulping mucus and tears. She continued to read—it seemed to her husband to be a sickness with her—despite him during those hours he was away being a man among men. For his part, he respected and almost feared those sinews of character she retained, but resented them. "My wife's a great reader," he would boom among the husbands of cake-makers. It gave him cachet, he suspected, and somehow atoned for those moments when, with him biblically ranting, Old Testament sexually referring, she would laugh at him. He was a

18

violent man, but imposed restraints that threatened to burst the blood out of his facial skin.

Jenner, who at sixteen should not have understood but nevertheless did, handed him his cup of tea and sat sipping and watching from behind the light of the lamp.

Young Fred was still sulking. He could wait till death for a formal apology from his father, who was sorry but could not say so, offering instead a kind of blessing with a supper hunk of bread and cheese. Fred took slow bites before deciding on speech. Finally: "Jilly Sweetman tells me there's government troops coming up this way to flush out the blacks."

His father, who had known about this for some weeks, who had privately and quietly officially requested, said, "Now there's a man's job for you instead of this rubbishing school. They're going to clear out the lot who've been raiding the coast farms. Drive them back north and west where they came from. Shoot the thieving bastards if they catch them at it."

"They're still around," Fred said, trying eagerly for paternal favor. "The fellows have seen them out near Dorahy's place. He encourages them, he does." Oh, the lad could spill the sins of others with horrible readiness. "And old Charlie Lunt's as well. Sugar and flour and things. Tobacco. They give them, I mean."

"Do they indeed?" asked his father, who knew.

His wife was silently stirring knowledge in with sugar and tea.

"Gin lovers?" Mr Buckmaster asked shockingly of no one in particular; but his wife who could have endured any kind of lover at all said mildly, "They're kind to them. They think they're people."

"People!"

"Yes. People. Christ's skin was probably as dark as theirs."

"My God!" Mr Buckmaster cried, inspecting her handsome intransigent features for irony. Christ was the New Testament revealed once a week by a minister who viewed him joylessly. He was presented as totally pale-skinned and it was to a white man they sang their whining hymns. "My God! Up north, you know, up in the rain-forest, hunting them down makes a pleasant way of filling in Sunday." It could be done straight after addressing his puritan white god. He enjoyed watching her wince. "What's the bag, eh, mate?" he pursued. "Ten? Eleven? Not as good as last week."

19

"Leaving them to rot," commented his wife, suddenly brutal and vicious with him. "Not even a hole in the ground!"

"Ach!" Buckmaster grunted. "You're like all the other women after all." He felt unexpectedly pleased with this discovery. "Sentimental and stupid. First to squawk if a party of them raped you, though."

"I've never squawked at rape," his wife replied calmly, putting the supper cheese closer to her son's friend, understanding his subtlety.

There was a frightful silence. Young Jenner blushed. Even young Fred, thigh doodler of private and particular yearnings, was finding the scrubbed veranda floor of savage interest.

"There would not be," Mr Buckmaster said finally and heavily, "room for much else." A winner, he felt, in front of Jenner's bright intelligent eye.

But the boy gave a last embarrassed gulp at his tea and said to the waiting room, "I must be getting back now." The innocence of his red hair was startling against his newly educated face. He stood up awkwardly and walked over to the landing uncertain whether to speak again would be the ultimate refinement in this uncivil war. But the wife spoke.

"Good-bye," she said to him. "Thank your mother for me, and come again soon."

Young Jenner smiled once more, stopped smiling and said good-bye. As he cantered his horse into darkness, he understood that the blows dealt in metaphor were deadlier than the thwack of flesh on flesh. He could not ride fast enough to hear silence move in behind him while his soul lugged a new and doughy knowledge.

**D**ORAHY SUBMITS to this pull of fate.

He packs a small bag, noting how one's needs in age lie in inverse ratio to the expansion of the soul.

He hopes. He boards a lumbering coastal vessel that rocks him out of his capital and, after a sea-shaken slumber, wakes after the third night to a sugarville morning of hard blue and yellow north of the tropic. From the salty deck he observes the wide reaches of blue bay water as the boat enters his destiny. Coastal scrub has thinned out its scraggy imprecision and has become the scraggier, scrubbier buildings of a town he has not entered for twenty years, which yet, as he watches the houses grow larger with approach, fills him with a nauseating nostalgia.

He has kept apart as far as possible from the other passengers all the week, but now, as they join him along the railing, he feels obliged to share the excitement and the chatter. Hands point. Voices cry out. The boat noses its rusty way from harbour to river and river docks.

There are only two others disembarking and he hopes to avoid them, knowing the town is full of pubs. Their reason for return is the same as his and already, conscious of his ambitions for solitariness, he wonders why he has come. His elderly legs wobble on this Friday morning gang-plank but they are the same legs that strolled through this town twenty years before, and he marvels that he is experiencing grief when, he supposes, rage would be the better thing. Turning his back firmly on the river and the docks, he walks steadily up the slope past the warehouses and enters the town.

The streets are busy with horses and big drays. There are people on bicycles bumping along the rough roads. Groggy from all this, he stands uncertain in sunlight, his bag at his feet. One should never go back. He decides this with vehemence and wonders then is he thinking of the psychic mistake of it or his own lack of charity. One does go back, he knows, again and again. One should forgive places as much as people.

This place has much to be forgiven it.

Terrible to sense the valetudinarian legs tentative along the foot-path. But up here everyone saunters. He is relieved he does not look remarkable. It is a refusal to fight the heat which already is dealing him blow upon blow; rather a yielding to it. Already steam is rising from the baking township and its slow river. Already there is sweat along his hairline, the saddened back of his neck, trickling between his breasts.

He feels reluctant to face his hotel yet, knowing its drabness already, the tired pots of fern, the bar-stink, the narrow bedroom with its spotted mirror. He walks on one hundred, two hundred yards and finds a tea-shop sluicing out the evening before. Rinsing the last stains of it, a thin girl has been doing penance with mop and bucket. She couldn't care less about this elderly man with his thin face and thinner voice demanding tea. She isn't forgiving anybody, refuses the credit of his smile, while slinging her bile across one table surface after the other with a rancid grey rag.

But he tries.

"It's twenty years," he volunteers, "since I've been here." (Where are the banners, the bunting, the tuckets sounding at left?)

She deals savagely with the counter and crashes the glass jars of sweets to one side.

"Lucky you," she says.

"It seems to have changed a lot. You notice things after that time." But what has he noticed? Bicycles, drays?

"I don't." She is grudging altogether. "Don't notice any change, I mean."

"You're young," he says. "Things happen so gradually you never see them when you're young." Except for young Jenner, he remembers. Always remembering young Jenner with terrible clarity. "Coming back after a long time makes you see, pulls the scales off your eyes." He is conscious that he is talking too much.

Young Jenner sits opposite him at the rocky table and says, "Sir, do something. Please. You'll have to do something."

22

"Of course I'll do something," he says and the girl pauses with her slop-rag and says, "What did you say?"

"Nothing," he says. "Nothing." Jenner fixes him with his terrible grey young eye and says, "You mustn't hedge. You're the only one."

"Me?" He flexes his useless arms, thin at sixty and not much better at forty. "Boy," he says, "I could never have crossed the Rubicon. Never blasted my way across the Alps given an ocean of vinegar. But you are right, of course. It's the mind that does the blasting. I must apologise, boy, for never being one of your muscle-bound footballers with their intemperate logic. I never matched up."

"You matched up," says young Jenner. "Please don't apologise."

"Would you like," the girl asks, "a couple of aspirin?"

"No," he says. "No. I—it's the heat, you know. Come from the south. Feelings run warm here." And he frightens her again, because she moves away a little distance before asking, "What are you up here for then?"

"It's Back to The Taws week," he says.

"Oh that!"

"Yes, that. We're infesting in droves, I suppose. Migratory slaters crept out from under our little rocks. Full of sentiment."

"Sentiment!" she scoffs. "Sentiment! Well, if that's how you feel . . . My mum and dad talk about it. They're part of it."

He looks up to smile his gentle gappy smile.

"There must be dozens of us."

"Oh, yes," she agrees, and is kindly for a while with the dish-rag. "Oh, yes. My family came up here fifteen years ago just after I was born. They didn't do much good, though. I feel there must be something better than this. They're hoping they'll see old friends. They had a lot they'd like to see again. Who went away, I mean."

"I didn't have many friends," he admits, horrifying her; and young Jenner says, "Rubbish! Sorry, sir."

"Not rubbish, young Jenner," he says. "Not friends who mattered."

"You'll make me ashamed of you," young Jenner says. "I thought you always said it was the saints who mattered."

"I must have been talking through my hat, boy. Wise after twenty years. It was the moneyed men who counted. The power stars. The rules makers. I had all the wrong friends."

Jenner blushes. He is still sixteen and cannot handle the unintentional insult.

23

"Yes," Mr Dorahy goes on. "All the wrong ones."

He pays for his tea and the girl watches him curiously as he sips.

The courtroom begins to shift its walls inward.

Do you ever, Mr Sheridan was pursuing with deadly interest, take any of the natives prisoner for no reason and without their consent? Would it be possible in a patch of scrub, perhaps?

No, to your first question, Lieutenant Buckmaster replied. I only act on instructions.

And the second question?

No. I don't think so. You might on a station. Have a chance, I mean.

Without shooting them?

I suppose so, Lieutenant Buckmaster said sulkily.

But you said previously that shooting was the only thing they understood?

I suppose so.

Mr Sheridan smiled. Is it not very difficult, almost impossible, for a white man to take a blackfellow?

I think it is very difficult, but on an open plain, say, you might run a blackfellow up a tree and you would soon get him then.

Mr Sheridan took off his glasses, polished them and put them on again.

I want to know whether you could take them alive.

Hardly, Lieutenant Buckmaster said before he could pause to think.

Oh, Mr Sheridan said. Indeed! And he glanced through his lenses sharply at this portly young man and hated him.

Outside the courthouse a child began to bounce a ball against the timber walls. Mr Sheridan frowned.

"Well, that's it then," Mr Dorahy says pushing his cup to one side. Nothing stands between him now and the hotel. He gives the girl another smile and this time is repaid. Taking up his bag, he goes back into the sunlight and turns automatically in the direction he must go.

Brutally the sun underscores his age and the hopelessness of this return. The shops still look like shanties, but some beneficent council has planted palms on centre islands in the main street that takes him seawards. And the sea still burns its blue acid.

Beside the hotel office there is a group of people waiting. Like the remnants of some Eventide picnic, he thinks. There are faces he suspects knowing, pondering how "suspects" is the right word here. Semantic priss, he tells himself, examining cautiously the faces, the maps—boundaries changed, contours altered—of those near him. Gracie Tilburn had won first prize at the Liedertafel singing "O for the wings of a dove" which brought tears and the house down, and she is standing just ahead and to one side of him now with her blue bows and slender body vanished into rich fullness and plum silk. "How am I so sure?" he asks himself. There is an unforgettable mole that had once the magic of an Addison patch high on the left cheek bone. Nothing else is recognisable. Not to him. He hopes he is wrong, for there is still a splendour if only in his memory.

"Oh, Gracie, Gracie, Gracie," they had all warbled back at her afterwards, the choirs dispersed, the hall manager handing out weak lemon, the mothers sipping tea and crumbling biscuits.

Gᴿᴬᶜᴵᴱ ᴡᴬˢ a nice girl. She knew it. Everyone in town knew it. She had allowed only a remnant of her forces to be scattered by Freddie Buckmaster who would appear sometimes to walk her home after Sunday Bible hunts. That's what he called them, making her laugh her magnificent laugh so that her rather long nose quivered and her doric neck, which troubled Freddie deeply, would throb. He troubled her too, his loutishness, the very racketing quality of it coursing through her blood in a dangerous manner.

"And no boys, dear," her mother warned, along with a dozen other superstitious noli tangeres. "It will spoil your voice."

"Exactly what will spoil?" Gracie had inquired.

"I do not care to go into it," her mother said, but because she was superstitious felt obliged to add that, on the other hand, she had heard marriage enriched the voice, giving it darker tones.

"My voice!" Gracie admitted grudgingly, and already it was a burden. She suspected it was only a voice even though it was the best in those parts; and not until she had begun to soar her way through a jungle of butter-dish and cut-glass trophies was her assurance boltered.

Watching young Jenner the evening of the grand eisteddfod observing her with his lucid and innocent intelligence from four rows back while she sang, ignoring the bloody pianist, some of the loutishness in her, to which without any doubt at all Fred Buckmaster's loutishness had responded, demanded more than that cool-eyed attention. For a while she returned his gaze, buffet for buffet it seemed, and felt her voice superbly detached, the head notes so effortless and purely accurate that she was conscious of some spiritual victory not only over him and all those others jammed in the hall, but also over the terrible brown and green distances eating away at the compass outside.

Afterwards she had managed to be near him in the fragmented crowd.

"That was beautiful," he said with such simplicity she could only believe him. She was surprised to feel ashamed.

"She could go far," some thin man's back was saying to her parents. Far? She had heard of cities. But she knew then he meant distances of the mind, long pilgrimages of the spirit.

"Isn't that your teacher?" she whispered to young Jenner.

"You know it is." Jenner was observing her with interest. "What do you pretend for?"

"I don't know," she admitted. "I do sometimes. Everything here seems so narrow. So small. It extends the limits." She grew muddled. "Truly, I don't know." But she did in fact. She was claiming seclusion as well, an untouched-by-the-world virginality she thought might appeal. Jenner was too young to accuse fishers of men though he came close to it. His features were assuming the carved-out look of adolescence.

"I'd like to go far," she said. "A long way from here." She kept smoothing the silk over her hips.

"He didn't mean that sort of far, really," young Jenner said. "You always take yourself." He was recalling something from his last Latin lesson and the vision of Mr Dorahy with only adumbrations of despair viewing the hideous ochre landscape beyond the schoolroom windows.

Her mother knew she had calved a winner. She was a pusher of whacking determination, prepared to ram citadels for those bell-like top A's.

"Freddie Buckmaster is nothing," she later warned. "Tim Jenner is nothing. There are other things for you." She sweated through committees until someone arranged a fund.

"I'll be leaving soon," Gracie announced to the rivals who were resenting their collision on her courting veranda.

"How soon is soon?" Freddie Buckmaster asked, being desperate to prove something to himself before she went. He scowled. It only accentuated his thickish brooding good looks.

Gracie said vaguely, "In a few months. January or February."

"That's too soon," Buckmaster said. He had never heard her voice even at its most exquisite.

"That's too soon," said young Jenner, who heard only her voice.

Like the blacks, she could sing off disaster for him. His mother played the piano for her on those evenings when the Tilburns visited and Gracie, carelessly posed against one side of the unbelievable French grand that had been lugged battering miles from the south, decorated the long timber living-room with sound. It made a kind of truce between them, young Jenner and Buckmaster. Her throat affected them both.

"I could swallow her whole," young Buckmaster admitted. "Keerist!"

"It's her voice I want to gulp," Jenner said.

When he told her that he scored a sort of victory. She rode over to his home more often, a lazy-daisied hat flapping upon her shoulders. They wandered through grass-drench to creek banks where they would sit idly watching tiddler stir or dragonflies hurtling across the surface. Rested her hand briefly in his.

Buckmaster sniffed them out sometimes, perched on his tall and spying chestnut. He had chucked school and had moved into the police where muscles and dad had won him preference. His horse could feel the irritation in his rider's flanks.

"You'd better be moving back," he would order, having no finesse. "We're on the track of the bunch that raided the mill. My boys are following a little way back." His buckle shone. His belt shone. Some official silver buttons shone. "Tirra lirra by the creek," young Jenner said, smiling.

"Now what the hell does that mean?" Buckmaster asked.

He was ripe for revenge.

He crept on young Jenner one evening of long lilacs and bronze as Jenner came from the School of Arts with a bundle of books. There was no provocation, no time for specious gallantry, just the old bunch of fives smashing the nose bridge, the baffled mouth, cracking the ear till it screamed with the noise of deafness. Jenner, his visions torn, felt only bones commenting on flesh and, dropping the books in the dust, fought back with every part of him until Buckmaster, thudding his whole bull weight into his stomach, dropped him to the ground. Then he kicked him, once, with perfect timing and direction, so that his whole body wound itself up like a watch spring.

28

Mr Dorahy, coming down a back lane in his sulky, found Jenner vomiting by the side of the stock-and-station agent's storehouse.

"You're entering the world of men," he said. "Christ was wasting his time. It would take a score of Gethsemanes."

He took him home and cleaned the muck from his face and later, seated on the little porch, they watched the flattened scrolls of land-scape making proclamations until they were absorbed in a distant haze over which the moon rode clean and indifferent. Jenner kept repressing gouts of sobs which were shame rather than pain.

"Here's a man," Dorahy stated, "who might restore your faith."

A horse and buggy was clipping its way down the dirt road towards them, its driver a solid fellow and deliberate, a man from the back country who had once worked a barren and hopeless holding that he had tried to milk with half a dozen windmills. On the testimony of willow-twigs, he had believed implicitly in the presence of a great artesian source and had sunk his shafts with the same faith as a miner. In his half-finished shack he had waited the arrival of his girl. Drays drew north and then coaches and she had failed to step from either into the dream. It had been ten years and his letters did not tap her source either.

Now he had moved closer in, but his ill-luck followed. Ground he touched dried mysteriously. He had no luck with cattle, though he pumped from a creek, and his animals grew lean and ribby like the grass on which they fed. Yet he laughed from time to time, committed to help others who were luckier, begrudging them nothing he could give.

Taking tea now beside Dorahy and the boy, his chunky body was propped against the veranda steps. Moths were coming in, unsober with candle-light. Lunt lifted one delicately from his tea.

"And what were you doing in town?" Dorahy was asking.

"Just picking up a few things." Lunt drew deeply on his pipe. "A bit of tucker, some pipeline and a crank handle." But he seemed to have lost interest, even though hope still pummelled him.

He leant back to look at the boy. "How's your dad?" he asked. "He's been a great help to me over the years, did you know? Not that I like to lean. But you need a bit of a hand. That's when you sort 'em out."

"Sort what?"

"The real people. You see, I believed in that water. I believe in Eden. And I've tried to make one. But all the time I get the feeling the world's just a dream in God's eye."

What a hope, thought young Jenner, but he said wonderingly, "Maybe Eden's whatever you make. It's the trying."

Dorahy sighed. "Pliny had a heating system, you know, a water system, right through his farm home just a few decades or so after Christ. If he could do it then, why not you? Here. Now."

Jenner was moved by this idealism, but he could see it was mad impractical stuff. They couldn't put the water there.

"Did he now?" Lunt said with interest. "Yes. It was there all right. I only had to tap it. But it came in trickles like tears. It broke my heart when I knew there was enough of the stuff there to float a navy. A great inland sea of it. And now I'm not doing much better."

Even the landscape was isolate. Trees, floating moon.

"You should come by more often," Dorahy said, "and talk to me. God knows I need it. Is it very lonely out there? Any lonelier than here, I mean?"

"I still have mills," Lunt said simply, "sucking away at the creek. It's almost as useless as it was before, but each has a different voice and at night they yacker between themselves. Drive most people mad, I suppose, but they're good pals. They keep trying for me."

He pulled a bag out of his pocket and fished out a sandwich.

"You mind if I eat? Haven't had a bite since this morning. I'm giddy with the world."

"There's some soup going," Dorahy said. "I was just going to have some with Tim."

His kitchen lay at the back, a feverish little lean-to with a small wood stove backed up against a sheet of iron. Heat became personal here. There was a dresser with three cups, a few plates and half a dozen beautifully polished knives and forks that he kept in a box. The small sitting-room expressed its soul through a mass of books and candle-light.

Dorahy was ahead of them looking out the back door where he spoke to a darkness that moved.

"Who's there?" he inquired of a shifting twilight.

Standing by the water-tank, Kowaha showed up in the chiaroscuro of the oil-lamp, the pretty bluntness of her face shining in planes and

30

gentle arcs. She smiled merely and Dorahy, shoving his own face into lamp-light, asked, "Kowaha? What is it?"

Stuffed with shyness she could not speak. Stood staring up at him on the top of his steps, giggled a moment, staring at him and the two darker figures who had come in behind him. The solidity of them frightened her.

"You want tucker?" Dorahy asked then.

She shook her head and he was conscious that she was holding something.

"No tucker. Then what?"

She gestured with the bundle in her arms.

Swinging the lamp, he went down to the yard while the other two, breathing in dust and dark, stood waiting.

"What is it, Kowaha?" Dorahy asked, peering down at the coiled arms of her.

She held the bundle forward suddenly so that he could see the tiny child within, fuzzed and sleeping. She did nothing but smile, holding the child up for the three of them.

"Already?" Dorahy murmured. "Your baby already?" He had not seen her for several weeks.

She was pleased with herself.

Dorahy put out a careful finger to touch the sleeping face and breathed, "He's beautiful."

"Girl," she said. Laughing at his idiocy. "Girl."

"You've come for this?" he asked. He loved the world. "To show me your baby?"

"Show baby."

Lunt and young Jenner, male-abashed before the marvel of it, stood back in shadow.

"My friends," Dorahy said. "Tim and Charlie. But you know Mr Lunt, don't you?" She giggled at him again.

He was hesitating, searching for some commemorative thing that might be spelled out concretely.

"We must give your baby a present, eh? For luck. For lots and lots of it," he added, swinging round to the boy. "But I don't know what. I simply don't know what."

In the house Kowaha squatted on the floor above the child. It lay naked and kicking gently, frail, its skin a tender gold. Kowaha gurgled down at it.

"I have one thing," Dorahy mused, moving into the bedroom and shuffling through drawers. "Only one thing she might wear." He pulled out a little leather bag from which he drew a silver medal. "How about this, Kowaha?" And he handed her a small dulled disc with the arms of Trinity College, Dublin, insanely shimmering in the oil light.

"Classics," he said to young Jenner. "My final year it was. I knew there'd be a use for it."

Kowaha held the medal gingerly, lifting it up and smiling, then running her fingers over the embossing.

"For luck," Dorahy said. "It used to be my luck. In a way. I give it to you."

"Luck," she repeated.

He threaded it with a strip of leather thong. Then he bent down and placed the circlet over the baby's head.

"Little girl," he pronounced and he wasn't laughing about it. "Classical first."

Mr SHERIDAN re-enters Dorahy's mind, which is boiling in this crowded hotel. He is sitting back as the others register. His gentleness is fraying.

Do you ever receive warrants against blackfellows guilty of offences? Sheridan asked.

Lieutenant Buckmaster shifted his weight from one foot to the other.

Very few. I have received two.

What do you do with them?

I try to execute the warrant and, if I am not able, I send it back again.

Where do you send it?

I send it back to the Inspector General of Police.

Would it not—Mr Sheridan's pencil began a slow tap—I repeat, would it not be much better that the warrants for this part of the country should remain in your possession so that you might be able to execute them as occasion offers?

I have got copies.

You have?

A copy is sufficient, Lieutenant Buckmaster replied sullenly.

Then, Mr Sheridan said leaning forward, do you know of a great many being in existence for various offenders? Copies, I mean, of course. What, if I may ask again, would you have?

Only two, Lieutenant Buckmaster said. The bouncing ball outside reached towards a window.

Sergeant, Mr Sheridan ordered, remove that child.

Two? he pursued. I thought perhaps there were three. What are the two you have, Lieutenant?

I know of one for Wilson. He paused.

Yes? said Mr Sheridan gently.

The bouncing stopped. Inside the court they could hear the gruffness of the sergeant. Mr Dorahy breathed ironically, Suffer, imperative, little children! It was all a question of a misplaced comma.

And one for Kuttabul Tommy.

For what?

Attempted rape.

And the third?

There was no third.

I think there was, Mr Sheridan suggested. You acted as if there was a third.

No, Lieutenant Buckmaster insisted.

Do you not know of one for Mr Lunt's blackfellows?

Mr Dorahy from the body of the court noted with interest Buckmaster ease his thick fingers about his collar.

There was no warrant.

But you acted as if there were one?

Perhaps.

For what? Mr Sheridan asked, softly, so that Dorahy in the thickening fetor of the little court had to strain to hear him.

The murder of a gin.

But, Mr Sheridan said irritably, the murder took place after you acted, not before. Is that not so?

I don't understand, Lieutenant Buckmaster said.

You will, Mr Sheridan assured him.

At this point the assistant magistrate intervened.

There was a coroner's report, he said. Was it that you heard of?

I'm not sure, Lieutenant Buckmaster replied sulkily.

Are you or have you been liable, Mr Sheridan went on, in the course of your patrol to meet any of Mr Lunt's blacks?

It is possible.

Of course they keep out of your way if they know you are after them; but if they came within your reach you might meet them?

There might be a chance—a very little chance.

But there was no actual warrant, was there? It had not been decided by whom this gin had been murdered?

Lieutenant Buckmaster declined to reply for a moment.

Mr Dorahy leant trembling against the hard arm of the wooden bench.

We will return to that, Mr Sheridan said. Tell me, he inquired, fixing his Bible-stained eyes on the sweating lieutenant, do these blacks not cross to the coast?

It is possible.

And make their way to the island?

It is possible.

I understood you to say earlier in your evidence that there had been one complaint by Mr Barnabas Sweetman and another from Mr John Watters with regard to depredations on their property?

Yes.

Then you were informed by Mr Sweetman what tribes had done these things?

Yes. He mentioned the tribe.

And are you going to tell us what tribe it was?

Lieutenant Buckmaster shifted his feet which felt larger than the world.

The Lindeman tribe.

Ah, said Mr Sheridan. And do you know, to change the subject a little, of other cases of rape besides that which you have mentioned? His interest was terrible to see.

Not exactly rape, Lieutenant Buckmaster replied. But assaults on little girls at Bingin and an attack on a woman at the Mulgrove station.

Their eyes met and held.

Do you think the crime of rape is common among the blacks? Is it on the increase among them?

It is on the increase as they become civilised.

As they become civilised? That is a strange answer, Lieutenant.

As they become civilised, the cases of rape become more frequent, Lieutenant Buckmaster repeated stubbornly.

You are suggesting that white customs lead to degradation in an observant other race?

I suppose so.

Mr Sheridan was feeling completely bemused. Idiotically he asked, Do you observe much mortality among the blacks?

Lieutenant Buckmaster blew his nose. There have been a number of cases since I came to the district.

Mr Dorahy began to laugh out loud. A great racking bawling sound escaped his throat.

Remove the witness, Mr Sheridan ordered without taking his eyes off Buckmaster.

S NOGGERS INTONED, interrupting some easy-chairmanship tralala at the end of the room, *Domine non sum dignus*, and there was an instant babble and quacking of agreement with him.

Bloody *thinks* himself, the chairman complained softly, unaware that Snoggers had publicly denied this. Order! he cried over his agenda sheet and unblotted papers. Order!

The council ripples petered out. The moment became a blemish.

Snoggers Boyd was the town's printer. He had found himself in this town more by accident than anything else, dedicated to bring out a struggling broadsheet weekly. Not one of the big men, but a necessary irritant. Not an active member of the Separation League, but a man who printed their agitations. He owned a pleasant home and a beautiful wife who had been in love, as far as he could judge such a private matter, for a few moments with old crumbling Lunt. During a crisis, his wife and Lunt had once held hands and at the moment, despite its brevity, Mr Boyd observed as well his wife's face full of unhappy movement. She had been nursing Lunt through a bout of pneumonia and the clasp of hands was permissible. She had never held his hand again, that he knew of, and he reverted to his cynical unwatchfulness.

"What we are here to decide," Mr Sweetman of the short dark curls and angelic playboy-manqué face said to his reordered henchmen, "is the punitive quality of our protests and the form they must take. Are we merely to restrain and hand over or are we to take action into our own hands?"

"Please!" he shouted above the dissonance then. "One at a time."

Mr Buckmaster rose. He had discovered the force of the eye which now he let move about the table, sifting the perhaps of those ten faces, each set in its own prejudice and bigotry. Man among men, he projected his strength into each watching face, even that of the town printer who had proclaimed his unworthiness. Bloody comic, thought Buckmaster. Aloud he said,

"This matter, gentlemen, is one that must hit deeply at the consciences of all of us." There were appreciating grunts. "A little girl—a baby, rather—removed from her mother's care"—he allowed a moist eye to rest for a moment on Benjy Wilson's face—"abandoned a week later in a state of filth and sick from lack of food. We are not interested in the whys of doing it. We are interested only in the fact that it was done. Fortunately she is all right now but that is not the main point, Mr Chairman. Not the main point at all. Are we to stand by while those things we cherish" (he thought briefly of son Fred and dismissed the thought) "are taken from us? And there is the matter of cattle, too. Part of our livelihood. The food for our children's mouths."

"Don't overdo it," said Snoggers, who hadn't learnt his lesson.

Swinging on him, Buckmaster cried, "By God you have a strange way of looking at things! We're here to determine fundamental attitudes."

Stubbornly Snoggers said, "I believe the blacks. They found Benjy Wilson's little girl about five miles from her home. They had no idea who it was. They did their best, damn it, to help and only left her out near Jenner's place when they found she wouldn't eat. Poor bastards," he said. "Give them credit. They tried."

Buckmaster was a bulging purple.

"We only have their word for that."

"And the Jenners'."

"Gentleman," Mr Sweetman interrupted, "it is the casualness of the whole affair. The irresponsibility. Are we to risk the continuance of this sort of thing? By our very softness allow it to get out of hand? This is"—he paused—"the thin edge of a very long wedge."

Snoggers's fat face swelled also. "They were being kind in their own way to that child," he repeated. "Kind. Are you going to take them to task for that?"

"There's the matter of six cows, some poultry and a horse," Buckmaster shouted. "My God! The horse alone demands reprisal!"

Snoggers said, "Count me out."

Buckmaster was still towering. This headless trunk of stone, the well-read Snoggers parodied to himself, stands in the desert. Jaysus!

"I move," Buckmaster continued, ignoring Snoggers as some kind of poltroon, "that we do not wait for a warrant from the south. It will take too long. I move that by next Monday at the latest we have prepared a punitive force, without sanction if you like—I repeat, without sanction—that will go straight to the scene of the trouble, sort out these blacks once and for all, taking whatever measures it thinks fit. Who's with me?"

Snoggers was almost trampled to death in the rush.

That's Lunt, dog-lonely after some brief supper of potatoes and beef boiled to rupture point over his vindictive stove. He's a front-step sitter and a reader of old papers that come by chance wrapped around his stores. He would be lonely but for his dog, the rusty strainings of his mills, and the hungry stirrings of his stringy cattle in the home paddock which translate him into a state of acquiescence. His lust for charity is eased by the gentle attentions he gives his animals, feeling guilt over his own supper when they low in hunger. He hand feeds them when he can afford it, waiting for the mills to tap their sources as he had waited for his girl. But that was another place, another time, and yet he seemed to bring ill-luck with him, for nothing thrives. All country has its black spots and he appears doomed to settle innocently on them.

But he read aloud to his dog and the great black shapes of the mill-monsters against the early evening. Vegetable prices in Brisbane are up. The recent drought has been responsible for over-priced greens in the Moreton Bay area. A terrible crime at Gatton. Women teachers seek equal salary rights. Man suicides from northern fishing-vessel, Gladstone, Thursday, a man whose identity is still unknown.

Like me, Lunt said, looking up from the month-old paper. He announced this to the dog and the nearest mill, which waved mechanically back in acknowledgment. My identity is still unknown.

He threw a stick for the dog who looked at it for a minute, wagged his gratitude, and remained by Lunt's feet watching it in case it moved again. Lunt clicked his fingers for him and lit his pipe, and that was how the sporting town councillors found him, grave with twilight amid the loneliness of sail-creak and grass-stir. The sky was one huge bruise of wider and darker air. Sitting there still, one arm dangling,

39

Lunt watched them through the home gate, their horses high-stepping through tussock. Then Mr Sweetman, who was leading, trotted smartly through the clearing and came up to sling his reins loosely over a veranda post. Buckmaster trotted after him and, totally at ease, the two of them made themselves at home on the veranda steps while Lunt expressed surprise or pleasure. The doubt was in him.

"It's a bit of a step up here, Charlie," Sweetman said. "You're pretty cut off."

"That's how I like it," Lunt said simply, straining at them with his tired eyes through thickening twilight.

His visitors' eyes were polished and active, saw night-fires a mile away by one of the water-holes, absorbed this and chewed at it while Lunt poked round his kitchen doing things with kettle and cups. These were firm on their saucers when he brought them out. His innocence was impregnable. He apologised once for not being much of a social cove and sat opposite them with his pipe going.

"You've got some company, I see," Sweetman observed, his eyes still on the patch of fire. "Down on the outer run."

"Just a few blacks down at one of the water-holes. Poor devils. You take sugar?"

Sweetman took sugar but his mind persisted sourly.

"You had them here before?"

"Sometimes. Off and on. They don't give any touble. Beg a bit of tucker now and then. I don't mind. Someone to share with."

Mr Sweetman shared Mr Buckmaster's eyes for a minute. Words were clogging their mouths and had to be spat out.

Finally Buckmaster said, "It's like this, Charlie. You can't be blamed. You don't know what's going on the way you're stuck out here, only coming into town for the odd day once a month, but these bastards have been behaving like animals. Beyond the law. Just like bloody animals."

Lunt decided not to enter a debate of such minimal invective. His eyes widened.

"Racing off with that kid, Benjy Wilson's little girl. Cropping off Ted Spiller's cattle. It's got to stop."

Sweetman kept making assenting sounds and movements that welded him, in a twinning of ideals, Lunt thought, to the other man. Lunt had slow eyes. A slow face. He looked up carefully over his tea.

40

"What actually happened to the child?" he asked slowly.

Buckmaster began an incoherent raving.

"Let's get this straight," Lunt suggested when the maniac paused. "The way I heard it in town, she was lost and they found her. Was she harmed in any way?"

This was not at all the way the conversation should be going. Buckmaster wanted unhinged loyalties.

"Half-starved, that's all!" he roared. "Isn't that enough?"

"No," Lunt decided after a long pause. "It's not enough. She wouldn't have eaten their sort of food. Perhaps that's why they were forced to steal."

"Oh, Jesus!" Buckmaster cried. "You'd excuse Judas."

"I might," Lunt agreed. "I might. Can I top up your cup?"

About them sudden dark. All the threatening black of the tenth station, a medieval obscurity for the town fathers who squatted like powers and principalities. Time for a Miltonic sweep of wings. Lunt watched them both with a half-smile they failed to decode and was conscious above their looming shoulders of restless light against the far sky.

"Polluted man," he said.

"I don't follow you," Sweetman said, "but I do know this. We want your help. You know these people. We're forming a party to round them up and move them out. If you'd join . . ." His voice held an especial note of pleading. "But we don't expect that. In respect to your niceties, that is. But you can help, you see, by saying nothing. Not preparing them."

"I won't do it," Lunt stated flatly. "These aren't the ones. You've got the wrong bunch altogether."

He was definite with his pipe. Refilled the kettle and stood it back on the stove, feeling the security of the banal matters of living crumble. Even the kettle rocked.

"We have proof," Buckmaster said through spittle.

"What proof?"

"Proof enough. I don't have to go into it, by God! They were seen."

"I see them also," the stubborn Lunt said. "I see them every now and then. If they'd had a child with them, a white child, in the last month, I'd have known."

"How?"

"By God, I don't have to go into it either! I simply know."

"Then you refuse?"

"Of course I refuse."

Sweetman tried placation. He said, "Think it over, old man. Don't make a sudden decision on a sentimental basis. We all do that."

Buckmaster, repressing, felt his face would split open.

"You're one of us," he was going on stupidly. "You have to see things like the rest of us."

"I don't think so." Lunt answered his kettle's summons. "I don't think so at all. I only have to see things the way I see them."

"Then you will warn them?"

"I'll do whatever I think proper."

"You'll regret this," Buckmaster threatened.

"No. You don't understand," Lunt said. "You never regret obeying conscience."

"Christ!" Buckmaster said. "You're mad. Mad mad mad."

In the heart of the next morning, under its early carnation sky, Lunt and his dog went round to the horse-yard. The mills were creaking, straining their guts to drag trickles of love from the red powdered earth. The land lay flat all round with its dusty scrubby shade trees making black dawn patches.

Lunt bent down and took a pinch of dust between his thumb and finger, sucked it and swallowed.

"Ah, you bitch country," he said. "I love you."

The dog trotted beside the horse across the mile stretch to the dried-out river where the camp lay. Lunt sang as he rocked in his saddle, out of tune and kindly towards sky: "This man comin', this man goin', earth stay flat and here. This man comin', that man goin', woman stay warm and here."

He laughed in his middle years at his craziness, and was still smiling when he rode into the camp and smelled the first of their fires. The dog shot away from him to bark at the blacks' dogs, circling them, then coming in for a snap and tussle. Three black men stood silent by the edge of the big water-hole watching him down the slope, watching his horse pick over the rock outcrop. The black faces shone as they saw him but it was only the sun striking up and over the coast range.

"Morning," Lunt said, and then greeted them in the few words he knew of their native dialect. They grinned at him and he rubbed his

42

hands along his thighs, slid from the saddle and asked, "You fellers got tea?"

They nodded. Over their shoulders he could see two of the women squatting in front of the fire. A baby howled at their side. The morning was full of awakenings.

He dipped into their billy with his saddle mug, squatting also with the women who smiled and turned away. The men had not yet spoken, but he knew them both—old Bunyah and Kowaha's tribal husband, a splendid tall fellow called Koha.

He knew these things took time, so he sipped a little. The baby yowled again and was picked up to drag on a breast. Crooning sounds came over the fuzz of its skull. My God, he thought with reverence, they've grown from the earth. Straight from it.

Finally Lunt asked, "You have any trouble down here last night?" The tea left a bitter taste in his mouth. Or perhaps it was the dust still. His tongue felt troubled.

Bunyah came to squat beside him. He was fighting for the words. "Two feller. Horses. Dogs. Tell us move bloody quick time."

"We say," Koha added, "Mister Lunt leave us stay. He know us feller long time. Bin stay fish and things."

Lunt smiled. "They have a story," he said. "Think you took Benjy Wilson's little girl. Did you?"

"Gawd, no, boss!" Koha laughed. "Whaffor? One piccaninny here already."

"They mean business," Lunt said. "They're crazy men. They'll come again, with guns maybe, shoot you down, women and kids. What will you do, eh? What the hell will you do?"

Koha made a little dust-picture with his big toe.

"Can't move yet," he said. "Old man sick and still plenty fish this hole."

"But your women, your kids?" Lunt said. He felt hopeless.

"You help, boss?" Koha asked. He had his gods and was innocent about them.

All their faces were dark with waiting. Three other men had come up along the creek-bed. They had two more gins and a couple of half-grown children with them.

The carnation, meanwhile, had run out of the sky and the sun was up.

"Of course."

"What, boss?"

"Yes, I said, yes. I'm warning you now, aren't I?"

He felt desperate under the malice of the rising sun. One man, one rifle. They'd be back in the evening with guns and dogs. It would be a massacre.

"I think," he said slowly, "you ought to move back for a bit. Little way. Back towards the hills. There's more cover. By tonight, anyway. You can come back here when the chase is off." Koha was struggling with white-man talk.

"Move long time?" he asked hesitantly.

"No," Lunt said. "No. Move short time. Seven nights, maybe. But today. You can leave old Tiboobi with me. I'll look after him."

Koha stirred more dust with his reflective toe. He looked down at the patterns he was making.

Finally he said, "Gawd, boss, he no stay any time long you. He want come with us, his own people. He sicken more here."

"What's up with him?"

"He good-oh," Bunyah said. His age and dignity and curative powers were challenged. His old wrinkled skin shone brownly in the morning light.

Koha spoke rapidly to him in his own tongue, consonants straggly as eucalypts.

They're straight from the earth, Lunt thought once more, remembering how he had sucked that mother, tasting her on his tongue that very morning. For a flashing second another world was manifest, a lost and almost forgotten place of blue chairs and white mats and river-stirred curtains. Impossible. He wrenched himself away from the memory to follow the two men to a branch and bark humpy where Tiboobi hunched his illness under leaves.

The old man was gasping in his sleep and Lunt, bending over him, felt the roar of temperature from his body, heard the barriers within his lungs.

"He's got pneumonia," he said to the two black men with him. "You can't shift him. He'll die."

They stared blank.

"My God!" Lunt cried, raising his voice. "Devil disease. In here." He struck where he imagined his heart might be. He coughed for them. He gasped for air along with the man on the bed of leaves.

44

"Two days. Three. Unless I nurse him. Bring him up to the house."

They still stared. But Bunyah was beginning to frown.

"You heard me? You bright boy, Koha? You love this old man. You want him living long time?"

Koha nodded.

"You bring him to the house then, quick smart."

He backed out of the rough shelter which was made as much with love as with boughs and straightened up.

The old man groaned once more. "You bring him," he repeated, and did not look at the other two again.

It had taken him years to learn what the law had never learnt, that the best boomerang to use against them was the threat of silence.

Two of the younger men carried him there on a stretcher of stringy-bark. Half an hour had gone by before they capitulated to the threat of Lunt's sturdy back riding away without another word.

Lunt put the old man in his own bed, looking down at the black face against the torn white pillow. A bad anthropological joke. The tribesmen shuffled and were reluctant to go.

"Off now," Lunt commanded as gently as he could. "Off quick time. Look after your women."

Koha bent to lay his head against that of the sick man.

"I'll take care of him," Lunt reassured, "as if he were my own father."

Though there wasn't much he could do, he thought, as he watched the men, pigeon-toed and splay-footed, walk back through dust in the direction of the camp.

He sponged the old man down and rubbed in some chest embrocation he hadn't used for years. He fed him sips of cooled boiled water with aspirin mashed in it and sat by him and waited for the fever to go down.

At sundown the old man was worse, sitting up in the bed with his eyes turned in, the whites showing. Cries and moans of the fever-spirit were gabbled out, the congestion in his lungs thickening each sound. Lunt opened a tin of soup and heated it while the sick man babbled wildly. Having drunk it at a gulp he went back to fanning and sponging the dried skin and holding a blanket round the racked shoulders.

There were no smoke-lines by the river that evening, no cobber glow of fire. Somehow the camp had slipped away in the early darkness and as the light turned blue and became star-scarred, he was glad that one thing at least had been secured, even as Tiboobi raved in the crisis.

Near ten he heard the horses go past. They were walking them, but he still heard the soft slurring of dust as they went round by the far paddock, the clink of a bridle, a snort from a horse. The dog stood braced by the veranda steps, his urge to bark stilled by his master's hand on his risen fur.

Not long, Lunt thought. Not long before they're back. He watched the hands on his alarm clock staggering round for ten mintues, fifteen, soothing the old man as he cried out, forcing more water between the thick lips. The frizz of Tiboobi's skull was grey. His heavily ridged hands clawed at blanket and tribe memories of the green coast.

Lunt was praying for him when the horses came back.

The men came in without ceremony, riding-boots heavy on the veranda boards.

Barney Sweetman's angel face loomed over Lunt where he sat beside the stretcher and five other faces glowed in the darkness beyond the lamp.

"You bastard," Sweetman said. "You rotten bastard."

Lunt said nothing. Buckmaster shoved through the door past a fringe of rifles.

"What's this then?" he demanded, staring at the old man on the stretcher. "What the bloody hell is this, eh?"

"Lower your voices," Lunt said quietly. "The old man's dying."

"By Jesus!" Buckmaster cried, whipping himself up for violence. "Then I'll help him on his way."

Suddenly and dreadfully he raised his rifle and blasted through the black man's chest.

Lunt sat there in the pathetic splatter of blood, still holding the old man's bony body against his. His hatred for the men in front of him filled the whole of his throat and banged in his skull.

"He would have died anyway," he said. "You swine."

He laid the body back on the bed. The stained sheets took on a brighter hue.

"Where are they?" Buckmaster asked. His mouth was still trickling the saliva of his excitement. He felt a tightening in his groin. He found himself levelling his rifle at Lunt who smiled now, and the smile was the thorn in the other man's skin.

46

"I have nothing to say," he said simply.

"You're the law!" screamed Buckmaster. "So you are the law! Where the bloody hell have they gone?"

"I'm not," Lunt said with finality, "saying a bloody word."

"Oh, Christ!" Buckmaster whimpered. "Do you want a massacre! Let's fix the bastard."

Sweetman uttered a Judas "Sorry, old man" and the rest of them seized him then. One of them went outside and brought in some saddle ropes and although Lunt fought them back a rifle butt knocked the sense out of him and they lashed him strongly with a lot of unnecessary rope to the dead man and then both of them to the bed. Face to face. Lunt lay with his lips shoved into flesh already cold.

DORAHY LIES on his narrow hotel bed and thinks of Charlie Lunt. Waiting round to register amid a bunch of old-timers in the lobby, he had stood apart from them when he could. Palsy-walsy, those others, clustering almost recognisable beside the pub's weary potted ferns with quick reminiscence, those tiny sparklers of recalled friendship cultivated for the seven-day stay with "We'll keep in touch" to keep them going.

How old would he be now? Dorahy wonders, remembering finding him, riding out there at the end of the week with the slaughters at Mandarana still a fresh stain. Afraid to enter because of the stench, and then seeing it, hearing the dead whimper as the dog snarled from the back of the room. A job more than he could stomach, but he had done it. Somehow. The ropes sunk deep in flesh by now, cut and falling away and Lunt dropping off the stretcher onto the floor with the terrible reek of his black companion stuck to his clothes and face.

Lugging him into the buggy, then, and saddling up, the dog as inert on the buggy floor as his master. Glancing back at the sunken face beside the dog's skeletal head and imagining—was it?—that once he heard the word "Thanks."

Young Jenner peers round the door of the bedroom, his face adolescent earnest, and says, "Sir, he's getting better. My mother says it's a miracle."

"Who did it, boy?" he asks.

"He won't say," young Jenner says. "Mr Buckmaster says it was the blacks did it."

"Desecrate their own?"

"He says it was a punishment for killing the old man."

"And what does Mr Lunt say?"

"He won't say anything."

"What a world!" Dorahy thinks. "What a world!"

He crosses to his window and looks out. Town looms out of rose. He marvels at the static quality of buildings he remembers, still there but nursing different memories for other eyes. He walks out to the veranda in front and looks down the road to see the school, extended and gardened, yet with a remembered window through which he had eased his mind while stumbling translation pocked the unreality of tropical summer. He can see the irony of it better now, the folly of discussing Hannibal's passage to power in this scraggy landscape that bore the frightful sores of its own history, scenes Suetonius would have regarded with horror—shattered black flesh, all the more horrible because of the country's negation—none of your soft olive groves and dove-blueness in the hills—heat, dust and the threat of scrub where trees grew like mutations.

Yet *Vivamus, mea Lesbia, atque amemus* put up alongside the scrabblings and the gropings, the arrowed hearts and linked initials behind the School of Arts, wasn't so different at that. Thinking of the slender boys bedewed with odours and remembering young Jenner in love with the slender ghost of the fat woman he had recognised in the lobby. Where, unable to rest, he feels that he must return. He unpacks his bag and hangs his other suit in the wardrobe. Womb-fluid is all nostalgia, he tells himself, walking back down the stairs, his puritan mouth keeled over towards disapproval.

At the foot of the stairs a man is waiting.

Dorahy looks uncertainly at a face whose features have been bashed by two decades of living since he last saw it. A name struggles to the surface and he knows who it is. There is nothing to this man now: a cipher once he had been washed up and let die.

"It is Tom Dorahy?" the lips ask.

"Yes."

"Remember me?"

"I'm terribly afraid . . ." He is battling to gain time. The lost shiftiness of the face disturbs him. He finds himself shrinking.

"Barney Sweetman," the old man says, confirming what Dorahy knows. "There isn't too much the same, but I'd know you."

49

Grudgingly Dorahy puts out a hand and has it pumped for a few seconds while Sweetman's down-and-out angel face crawls into his for deliverance.

"I remember," Dorahy says at last. "Things were different then. Are they any different now, I wonder?"

"A lot," the other says, and they both recall the high rock and the court and a certain hot noon. "Yes, a lot." Sweetman pushes his mouth into a smile. "I've cut right out of municipal politics altogether now. I'm still State member for this area. Gives me a wider interest. And there's no real retiring age, you know. A man has to do his work. You retire when the electors tell you and not a day before."

"And they haven't told you yet?"

"Still the same old Tom," Sweetman says, grinning. "You haven't changed, mate. No. They haven't sent me out yet."

"And Buckmaster?" Dorahy asks. "Buckmaster and his now middle-aged bull son?"

"Buckmaster's still here," he says. "But his boy pulled out of the police and runs a pub on the Palmer. A fine man he's turned out, so it happens."

"My God," Dorahy says. "My God!"

Sweetman places his arm around the thin shoulders for a moment. "You've come back, Tom," he says. "What's your reason then? You shouldn't have come back in a spirit of criticism. That's all over now. So long ago no one remembers."

"I remember."

"You won't forget, you mean. Are growing pains the only things you recall, eh?"

"Is that how you dismiss it? Growing pains!"

"Then why have you come back?"

"In the spirit of curiosity."

"I hope that's all," Sweetman says. "I've come along specially to meet you." ("Forestall," Dorahy thinks) "as part of the old place, to ask you round for a drink tonight before the official welcome next week. You'll be in that, won't you?"

Your lousy vote-catching manner, Dorahy thinks. "I'll be there," he says.

"Where's Charlie Lunt these days?" he asks.

Sweetman's face closes over. "Old Charlie," he muses. "Finally gave up that property of his. It was falling apart. He never did strike enough water."

"He lost heart?" Dorahy prompts.

"You could say that."

"He could have said more," Dorahy whispers. He feels very old suddenly. The girl behind the desk is watching them both. He is incapable of giving her a smile.

"Where is he then?" he persists.

"Somewhere up the coast," Sweetman answers at last. "A little mixed business. Better for him. Look after Mr Dorahy," he says swinging towards the girl behind the desk. Pulling rank. "He's one of our more important guests."

"Certainly, Sir Barnabas," she says. It sounds incredibly comic. She sighs too, Dorahy notices, and he thinks, "Ah by next election he'll know what it is to be told. He'll know all right."

"Have a bit of a kip, now, Tom." Sweetman uses a patting action on the other's shoulder. "You could do with a bit of a lie-down, eh? And we'll see you tonight about eight. We're still at the old place. Bit bigger, bit smarter, but much the same. You know me. Nothing grand."

Mr Dorahy has his lie-down.

HOW MANY men, Mr Sheridan asked Lieutenant Buckmaster, are there in your detachment?

Ten.

Ten official members?

The lieutenant squirmed. No.

Then how many?

Four official members only.

And were the men who accompanied you on this third expedition the same ones we were speaking of before, those same ten, official or not?

Lieutenant Buckmaster hesitated. Not all.

Who else, then, was with you on this expedition?

A few of the townsmen.

A few?

A few.

By what authority did they accompany you? I assumed they were armed.

I was sent for by Mr Romney.

Directly by Mr Romney?

Lieutenant Buckmaster shuffled something—his feet? his mind?

No, I acted on a letter received by one of the townsmen.

And who was that?

My father.

At the back of the court Mr Dorahy who had been readmitted to give evidence felt his lips in an unbearable twitch of a smile.

Mr Romney is a member of the Separation League, is he not? asked Mr Sheridan.

Yes.

Then he would know your father well—could be classed as a personal friend perhaps?

I suppose so.

What did you do, pursued Mr Sheridan, when you came to Romney's station?

I went first to the outlying properties and did not find any of the tribe there. Then I went towards the coast and followed it up to Tumbul. Finding no tracks there, I came back across the flats to Kuttabul where I discovered evidence that led us towards the Mandarana scrub. I found the blacks at the water-hole back from Mandarana.

What did you do then?

I dispersed them.

How did you know they were the blacks who had committed the thefts? Had you any direct evidence?

The boys at Mr Romney's told me these were the blacks. They said the tribe was in the habit of coming across their land to move south down the coast.

And that was the only evidence you had? Did you not, for example, recognise one of the gins who had been seen frequently about the town?

Come on, boy! Dorahy encouraged silently from the rear of the court.

The silence began to crackle.

Well, Lieutenant Buckmaster? Did you not recognise one of the gins?

The courtroom air was like a giant and fetid bubble of Freddie's blood.

No, he said.

For the moment, Mr Sheridan said, sipping at a glass of water beside him, let us leave that. Have you proper control over your troopers?

Yes.

But this group was not all native troopers?

No.

But you had proper control over the whole group?

Lieutenant Buckmaster began sweating again.

Well, Lieutenant Buckmaster? Had you control over the whole group?

I cannot really say.

Really *say*, Lieutenant? I put it to you that at one stage your troopers and the townsmen with you acted as separate entities.

That could be possible.

Had you given orders to the entire group?

Yes.

What was the nature of those orders?

I told them to go into the scrub and disperse the tribe.

Disperse? That is a strange word. What do you mean by dispersing?

Firing at them. I gave strict orders that no gins were to be touched.

And your orders were not obeyed?

To my knowledge they were.

But the group had split into two punitive forces, had it not?

Yes.

Then how would you know whether your orders were in fact obeyed?

Lieutenant Buckmaster offered silence.

Mr Sheridan's colour deepened. I must insist on an answer, Lieutenant Buckmaster, he said. If there are warrants issued then you are, I take it, acting correctly when you try to disperse or capture certain blacks. But in this case there was no warrant. I wish to know what induced you to give an order that could result in indiscriminate slaughter.

There was no—

Lieutenant Buckmaster, were your orders in fact obeyed?

I don't know.

I see. And do you think it proper to fire upon the blacks in this way in such circumstances?

They don't understand anything else.

How many bodies, Lieutenant Buckmaster, did you see when all—I repeat—all your forces rejoined?

I saw six.

Was there not a gin killed as well?

Dorahy leant forward against the rail in front of him, his face, his entire body, suffused with a kind of delighted anguish. He shouted, Yes yes yes yes yes, and for the second time that day Mr Sheridan had to ask for the witness to be removed.

\* \* \*

Lunt lay on his bed listening to the dust settle. Or thought he could.

Not the same bed. He had burnt that, dragged it out into a rose of fire made by the first of the failed mills. Listening for the strain of rope and water being spewed up its pipes, he substituted the satiric fire instead, dragged on the putrid mattress where still he could see some of his own hairs and the old man's. Such a marriage. Consequently he uttered some sort of prayer during the sheet and the blanket. His girl had never. Not ever. He would have laughed if it hadn't seemed unkind at the best and blasphemous at the worst.

So he lay, returned and nursed back to some sort of health, for he had lost a leg, severed at a southern hospital, and he stumped round on his new wooden one. The only true separationist, he told himself, grimly smiling at the sick joke. Gangrene had got him, had entered silently a minor graze below the knee so that the old man's poison had done for it. So he lay, hearing the dust move, and knew that soon he would have to be about the simplicities of living—the horses, the dog, his few scraggy cattle whose rumps were leaner than his own. What day of the week it was he wondered, knowing he should have smelled out Saturday with his heart.

He put on his breakfast. The effort of it. Sat munching some bran mash in milk and sipping tea—the terrifying comforting monotony of it—and saw from the edge of his veranda, a long way off, a horseman who turned into Dorahy trotting across the outer paddock.

Dorahy was being rational and categoric that morning with the sun finally up and classes week-ended. He was full of dour logic.

"You must take action." He tapped the wooden leg. "The whole town is aware of who and when and why. Don't let it settle."

"There's no purpose," Lunt said, sad for the other bloke who was so righteous in his pettiness.

"There's every purpose. This stinking tiny town taking people by the nose and then ramming them in their own filth—or worse, the filth of others. By God!" he breathed.

"They've gone now," Lunt said. "My squatters. My dark campers."

"There was a massacre," Dorahy said, "the very next day while you were gasping it out. No one wanted to tell you." He couldn't resist ill-tidings for the life of him. "But there was a bloody massacre."

Here, Lunt recalled, was an explanation for averted eyes during his convalescence, the clipped-off utterance. Remembering the point of light in a glass of water steady on a bedside table while truth somehow refracted around the steadiness of light. Lips became oblique as words.

But Dorahy was not oblique.

"Someone," he said, "Buckmaster, someone, lashed you to that bed leaving you to die."

"I'm unkillable." Lunt grinned for the folly of it while Dorahy stirred his tea angrily.

"The whole school is buzzing with it now that you've come back—like this." He gestured towards the wooden leg. "They're like blowflies buzzing over the dead meat of that week-end. The town. I'll stir things up, truly. There'll be a commission about this."

Lunt said, "That will only fatten their self-importance. They'll grow big with a commission. Let it rest."

"But it's not just you," Dorahy replied, wiping a trickle of tea from his long chin. "It's the old man as well. It's Kowaha. It's her husband. It's Kowaha's child."

"The child?"

"A miracle," Dorahy said. "I've been looking for one in this place. A blooming of Eden, as you say. They collected her, those vigilantes of justice. Some curiosity or oddity, they thought. The Boyds looked after her for a few weeks and now the Jenners have her. There's no one left, with the tribe scattered to buggery." The word sounded terrible on the teacher's tongue. He felt a vile taste and heard Buckmaster.

"I see," he remembered the other man saying, "the bloody kid came top in Latin! Some sort of prodigy, eh? You coach them younger and younger, Mr Dorahy?"

"She was more apt than the Lieutenant," he had countered.

Now he watched Lunt shift his good leg, rubbing at a stiff thigh.

"Please," he begged. "Please. Don't let them get away with it."

Lunt's clear blue eyes speculated on distance. The mills were un-moving, their arms dead wood. If only the water. It could be his salvation, that lost coolness.

"It could so easily have been us who did it," he said. "The luck of the draw. They carry their punishment inside. For ever."

"Ach!" Dorahy expostulated, mad with the need for retribution.

Young Jenner had fingered the silver medal on the baby's golden chest. It moved in tiny pulses. "She's a winner, sir," he had said. "You've given her your luck."

The timber house was full of heating air. Sun shafts became rapiers slashing the eastern rooms of the sagging building. Dorahy swung one like a cleaver. His arm parted motes.

"Whether you want or not," he cried, "there'll be an inquiry. Fred Buckmaster has to put in a report to fool justice. Oh, there'll be an inquiry all right and I'll speak if it's the last thing I do."

Yet at the time he gave only ironic yelps of laughter.

BARNEY SWEETMAN'S house skulks behind a mess of wattles.

Dorahy is unable to knock upon this door, for it lies open with a frankness that is devastating. At the end of a lighted hall he can see part of a big room filled with people and for a moment only is afraid for himself and the folly of his tongue. His entry into light has the manner of stage device, for the fifteen or so people who are there stop talking as he stands hesitating before them all.

Sweetman swoops.

There is a glass in Dorahy's hand suddenly and he is sipping amid cries of welcome that bring the bile acid to his mouth. He is clobbered silly by their greetings as they all lie and tell him he's hardly changed.

"I'm much the same inside," he says awkwardly—but it is really a threat—and this is a sardonic aid for those who talk only of externals. Something makes him want to cackle at their absurdity, but he sips again and the wine warms him. There'll be some kindness, he hopes.

"Part of the town," a fat man is saying about him with genuineness, smiling. Where had he seen that smile? In what agonised situation twenty years before?

"You remember the old Snoggers!" Sweetman cries, and Dorahy is grateful to be helped, feels the trembling start in the hand that holds the glass, and nods and says "Of course" as his eyes track beyond Mr Boyd, town printer, to the bullishness of what can only be Buckmaster, a ruined piece of flesh propped by the mantel.

"After all these years!" Buckmaster is crushing his hand. Dorahy does not want to take communion but it is there, offered with fabled obliviscence. "Why, it's like old times!"

All our eyes are smaller, Dorahy thinks. It reflects our nothingness. And he says, rather bitterly, "Not too much like old times, I hope," and watches for shadows.

"What's that suppose to imply, hey?" Buckmaster demands. But his smile is still in place. He is very lined and the wine that stained his cheeks once has now run its blemish all over his face.

"There were times," Dorahy says, resolving to be careful, "when we didn't see quite eye to eye."

"There were," Buckmaster agrees. "But that sort of thing isn't for an evening like this. Past is past, eh?"

Dorahy takes a larger sip at his drink and repressed anger. He wants to shout "Not ever" and whack the room apart with some claymore of accusation, but a certain smile on Boyd's face stops him. There will be other moments for that, the smile says, spelling out postponement—and he is puzzled.

"Where's Charlie Lunt these days?" he finally asks Buckmaster, to annoy him.

A knot seems to appear in the centre of Buckmaster's face.

"He moved up to the coast a bit," he replies. "Gave up his old holding."

"It would be pleasant to see him again," Dorahy says, remembering the room, the bed, the rope. "Is he well?"

Buckmaster shrugs and catches Sweetman's eye.

"He was invited," he lies. "He might turn up. Haven't seen him for years."

"But he should be here," Dorahy nags, forgetting his resolutions. He takes another gulp of his drink and feels a hugeness of just rage constrict his chest. "He's the most memorable part of the town."

"In what way?" Sweetman asks.

"A martyr. A saint."

"Oh, God, Tom!" Buckmaster says. "I thought you would be letting go by now."

"Saint Lunt," Dorahy intones, "appear and bless this meeting." His smile is lost in memories.

There are too many people in the room, even for its largeness. He is reintroduced to Romney and Armitage and Wilson and all the faces have a familiarity he is too tired to unmask, even that of Freddie Buckmaster who is lounging heavily against a window pane. He is confidently forty, now, and has a wife and two legal children.

59

Dorahy has another drink. And another. Mellowness or daring will set in. He corners Snoggers Boyd in an angle between living- and dining-room and asks again. "Where's Charlie Lunt?"

Boyd appears truly jovial, yet his mouth tightens and he says, "It wouldn't have done, I suppose, his coming."

"Why not, for Christ's sake?" Dorahy cries. "I'll fetch him. He can be fetched?"

Boyd sucks at his pipe, lips drawn back as he clenches his teeth.

"Come on now, Tom," he says.

"Is it possible?" Dorahy persists.

"It's possible he would be unwilling."

"Why?"

"Well, what good would it do? It's years too late."

"For justice to be done?"

Boyd frowns. "You're an impossible person," he says. "Lunt hasn't come near this place since he left. He obviously doesn't want to be reminded either. Who the hell do you think you are? Social conscience?"

"You're right, I suppose," Dorahy admits. "But I'd like to see him all the same. He was a truly good man."

"Let it rest a bit." Snoggers's eyes are sad. "If it's only seeing him you want, I might be able to arrange something. A run up the coast for you. I've been up there myself once or twice. How long are you here for?"

"Just the week."

"And why did you come?"

"You're the second person who has asked me that," Dorahy says. "Curiosity. That mainly. And a hope for delayed justice."

"That's the nub of it," Boyd says. "I feel as you do but I act differently. Have another drink."

He has another drink. And yet another. He allows his mouth to remain shut against anything bar social inanities, even to Fred, ex-lieutenant, who lounges across the room to examine him more closely. Buckmaster's soul grows bristles.

"You two yapping away here!" he accuses. "What is it? Conspiracy?"

Fred's crassness comes from the beer-pot belly-rumbles of secure middle age. He has a moustache horribly flecked with beer-scum. He grins at his former teacher and turns into a cartoon of himself.

"You haven't changed much," Dorahy says, referring to the soul.

"Nor you." It is as if young Buckmaster has caught on.

Boyd keeps smiling into his glass. He senses thunder on the left.

But someone in the room is calling for silence. Let's hear it for Sweetman who stands posed by a solid dresser holding out a toast glass like an Olympic runner's beacon. The conversation plays itself out in trickles.

"Old faces, old friends," Sweetman is throbbing as the party noises fade. "Welcome home. For it has been your home and will be as long as you remain." Cheers from some moron. "It is good to see so many of us reunited after all these years, though it is sad to remember those who cannot come. But here you are now seeing what the old town has turned into. Once, and you all remember that once, it was simply a village, a bit of a township. I mean no offence. But look around you over the next few days and you will see that what was once a township has turned into a thriving town of enormous economic importance for the southern States. Those of you who were with me in the Separation League know what this means. The implications."

He pauses to allow the implications to sink in. Boyd is again tempted to a liturgical *Domine non sum dignus,* but refrains and cocks a wink at Dorahy who is broodingly absorbed. He misses six platitudes and comes to to hear Sweetman, in a stage voice nicely broken between the kinetic properties of nostalgia and actual tears, talking about mutual love and respect, the necessity to pull together.

"Oh my God, the clichés," Snoggers whispers in an aside to Dorahy who frowns with his terrible righteousness and whispers "Twaddle!" back at him.

There are a few isolated bravos and an epidemic of clapping while Dorahy's hands remain firm around his glass. He is urged to shout down the fluff, the cobwebs of nonsense. It is not the time. He waits.

DORAHY THAT Sunday was filled with Godtide. He had observed the vigilante grouping of the men as he rode through the township on his way to Jenner's. It was a horrible boil-up of masculinity, he thought, as he passed them by, resisting invitation with a cool wave and shake of the head. He sensed bloody trouble, the smell of it, all the way out of town.

Mr Jenner was hoeing vegetables in a patch at the rear of the house. The peace of it was almost comic. He was a tall man with a crop of receding red hair and a frightening calm. So slow appeared everything he touched one nearly missed the steady forwardness of it.

Dorahy said abruptly, "They're on their way. What can we do about it?"

Jenner put his hoe down carefully and straightened up amid the silver beet.

"Who?"

"The men of God. The town elders. They're out on a black hunt, as I predicted yesterday."

Jenner seemed to be staring into lost distances. "What do you want to do?" he asked at last.

Dorahy found his mouth full of angry saliva.

"Go after them. See that no harm is done."

Jenner sucked at this idea for a while. He could have bitten straight through to the centred seed but preferred rumination, if only for the look of the thing.

"Two of us only?"

"Your son, perhaps."

"Three! Two men and a boy! They'd laugh in our faces."

"Some protest must be made."

"It will do nothing."

Dorahy frowned. "It puts our case. I had thought Boyd—but he was with them."

Jenner smiled. "But so feebly," he said. He picked up the hoe and began walking back to the house. Dorahy followed. Day was beginning to blaze. In such sunlight, which could eat its way through sinew and bone towards the soul, both men felt exposed.

"Still," Jenner went on as they neared the back steps, "I do see your point. I'll come with you. The smallest protest force in history. My God! But we'll achieve nothing, you know."

Tim Jenner was painting railings. The wife and daughters were seated sewing on the long veranda. The contrast of it made Dorahy laugh sourly at the thought of that ten-strong band of yahoos bristling with guns.

He said, "It will express our point of view. Our conscience."

"They'll find us a joke," Jenner said.

"It will prick them."

"So?" Jenner said. "That isn't enough you know. Not nearly enough."

Dorahy said, "I'm wanting more than that, if it's possible."

"What, then?"

"I want them to know the town is divided. That other opinions have force and must be taken into account."

"What a hope!" Jenner said.

From the bottom of the veranda steps Dorahy smiled up at the three women on the veranda. Putting the case to them, he asked what they thought. He had never believed that to be female was to be incapable of judgment.

Young Jenner put down his paint brush and said, "May I come?"

"I should hope you would," his father replied.

"Then that's all there is to it," the boy said. He would lose his simplicity with time. His face shone. He believed Dorahy to be always infallible. "Are we taking guns?"

"No guns," his father said. "That's the whole point."

They rode out together, the three of them, trotting steadily north to Mandarana, aware both of folly and the older wisdom of justice.

The men were moving in a solid formation after the trees thinned out on the slopes west of the peak.

They were aware of, though at the moment they could not see, the dark shapes moving ahead of them towards the rock-crops and the scrub on the eastern face. Lieutenant Freddie Buckmaster, slicker than paint in a too-tight jacket with wicked silver buttons, pulled up his big bay and called a halt. Manoeuvres, he was explaining to them. Tactics.

There were ten men of God with him that sweating noon, well-mounted, well-set-up fellows, muscular as their horses and dangerous as their guns. Pillars of the town. Not even the flies troubled them as they sat loosely in their saddles, their thighs gripping lightly and easily at their edging mounts.

"We'll split into two groups," Lieutenant Buckmaster said. He was enthusiastic and sullenly young. "If Mr. Sweetman would take the northern side of the hill with four of you, the rest of us will go round by the south and pin them in." (After all, he hadn't read his Hannibal for nothing and momentarily, crazily, in the tea-tree scrub, Dorahy's face and sour snaggle-tooth smile blazed at him above a chalky desk.) "If they take to the slopes, as I think they will, we'll tether up and follow on foot. There's too much shale for the horses." His face was set in firm lines. "The dirty buggers," he said.

Trees were mnemonics for more and more trees.

In silent cheers and leaves the two parties cantered off, Buckmaster senior taking his burly form after Sweetman.

Sounds now of hoof-rattle and leather-squeak in a thickening air of tenseness and anger leaking out of their sweating flesh.

They had dogs with them, too, yelping and barking in a pack hunt as the leader scented and took off after the odour of black skin glimpsed briefly a hundred yards away.

On the eastern side of the mountain trees became denser than the logic of their movements.

"My God!" Roy Armitage panted, drawing in beside his leader, "this is too bloody thick. We'll have to leave the horses."

Young Buckmaster chewed on this advice for another hundred yards. His thighs took a bashing in the scrub.

"You're right," he admitted. A whip of tree cracked his face half open and there was blood apart from the pain. "Tell the rest."

They crowded each other in the one small space, clumping their horses together, and unslung their guns. Their irritated skins were demanding retribution.

Dismounted, they crackled through the trees on the lower slope that swept up to the beige and lilac shadows of the peak. Bracken dragged at their boots and argued with them. In the distance there was the sudden scream of a dog.

"There they go!" Benjy Wilson was yelling and pointing through thinner scrub at the rockier patches of the lower mountain where a score of clambering bodies glistening in light were scrambling fast and scattered up the steep slope. It was apparent from below that there was nowhere they could go but up.

Lieutenant Buckmaster paused, held up a masterly hand for attention, then tamped a leisurely pipe while his men fretted in check.

"The others will be here in a minute. The buggers can't get away now."

"I believe," Benjy Wilson volunteered eagerly—and there was saliva—"they've some sort of ritual ground up top. It flattens out near the summit. They'll head for that."

"Catching 'em at prayer, eh?" Buckmaster grinned and drew suckingly on his pipe. He was a lumpy lad with all the confidence of a very average intelligence. "Listen a minute. I think I can hear the other party."

The dogs were in first and then the men who held a confrontation under the disturbed trees, glancing up now and then at the distant diminishing figures still stolidly climbing up to the peak.

Snoggers Boyd, who had come, despite his protest, for a variety of subtle reasons the others did not know about, said over Buckmaster senior's shoulder, "Let the poor bastards be. We've given them a run for it."

"Are you mad?" Buckmaster questioned. "They've got to take a warning. They've got to be dispersed. We're going up that hill. Are all rifles ready?"

"Not mine," Boyd said.

"Jesus! Well, fix it."

"No." Boyd was mopping his fat sweating face.

"What?"

"God fuck Ireland," Boyd said simply. "I said, no. And no again. I've had enough."

"You'll do what you're bloody told."

Boyd smiled. His fat was of the genial kind, but his eyes were sharp. "I'm not going to watch you," he said flatly, "butcher those poor devils. I don't know why I came except to see fair play. And watch self-righteousness in action."

"Well, go to buggery!" Buckmaster roared.

"Thank you," Mr Boyd said, "I will"—turning his horse on the word to trot it away into the trees to the north.

"Oh, my God!" Buckmaster cried, appealing to Barney Sweetman. "Are we ready, then?"

The others were dismounted, their rifles cocked. Over all the faces was a sheen of appetite for something. They had a foxish look under the moving tree light.

"Fan out!" young Buckmaster cried. And the men worked themselves into a straggling line about the base to begin working their way up the slope, their feet constantly slipping and crunching on stone and gravel, their lumbering bodies bent forward with the effort of it, sixty degrees in spots once they had cleared the scrub; but their steady climb took them slowly upward towards the flattened altar of Mandarana.

Fred Buckmaster kept his glinting eyes on possibilities slipping brownly away at the crest, and once, stupidly, he aimed and fired at what he thought was a straggler while his impulse released something in all the men who began blasting away at tree and rock.

"Hold it!" canny Sweetman roared down the line. "Oh, hold it now!"

They crawled up another two hundred feet and it seemed they had the mountain to themselves under this hot sun. The light was dry and brilliant. Nothingness was scarred by crow-cry, distant and sad. Only rock, scrub and the long line of fox-faced men moving in towards a massacre. They were only ten yards apart now as the cone of the mountain narrowed and could hear one another's snorting breaths and the clink of boot on rock.

Just before the ground began to level out, there came a shower of spears and stones, a poor volley that would have had Mr Boyd in tears for the poverty of its protest. The men ducked, lay on the baking earth, and reloaded.

"Fire!" Freddie Buckmaster ordered his troops, and the useless shot whined up over the crest while the rattle of the rifles died away as they still lay there a minute before scrambling on.

When they came over the lip, the ground stretched flat for several hundred yards to end in a random-slung boulder heap guarding the cliff edge on the western face. And nowhere was there any movement.

The men edged in towards one another, their eyes scanning the summit.

"They're in those rocks," Fred Buckmaster stated. He was categoric. "As sure as God made little apples. All we've got to do is flush them out."

They advanced slowly, still keeping to their line formation.

There were stupendous views out towards the sea behind them and in across the flats to far ranges. They ignored all these splendid airy spaces.

"Now!" Fred Buckmaster cried. And they broke into a run, whooping as they went towards a cleft in the boulders.

The world, the stupendous views, narrowed to a horror of shots and shouts and screams as they burst in upon the score of blacks herded into the inner circle of rocks. One spear caught Roy Armitage in the shoulder, but the others flew wide as the natives, awed by the bullet, became only a huddle of terrified flesh. They cringed against rocky shields. One old man made a break for the side of the rock circle, but Benjy Wilson brought him down with a bullet neatly placed in the centre of his spine. He lay moaning and twitching.

It was truly time to make arrests, but Buckmaster had lost control of his men who went forward and in, shooting steadily and reloading and shooting until the ground was littered with grunting men and there was blood-splash bright upon the rocks. Only five men confronted them now. The four or five women crouched wailing against the far barricade.

"Leave the gins!" Sweetman roared in a moment of sanity. "Leave them!"

There was a sudden silence and the five blacks still standing turned slow circles as they inspected the line of whites girdling the rocks. Words, at this point, failed. Freddie Buckmaster kept thinking, "Oh, my God! What now, what do I do now?" He really didn't know, having discovered blood and death. There was one gin he noticed, knew well by sight, having seen her on the outskirts of town. She was holding a baby closely against her breast and now and again it wailed.

"Make an arrest!" Barney Sweetman advised urgently. "For God's sake make an arrest!" He wanted things formalised. Already he interpreted the scene in terms of motions to be discussed and put, perhaps even as agenda.

Fred Buckmaster took a step forward. It was prize-giving day and the gauche fellow had never achieved such distinction before. His rifle was as limp as he. Some formal words seemed to be dripping from his mouth. The blacks moved back before him till they made a pitiful knot against his advance. He could see this pitifulness and the wretchedness of their defence so that some gland in him was disturbed to the point of his wanting to cry with shame.

And at that moment the gin whose face so moved him sprang with a tiny cry upon one of the rocks. Balanced there she looked in quick terror all about her and then, with no sound at all, hurled herself, still clutching the child, straight over the western scarp.

It was such a final gesture no one moved for a few seconds, numbed by the force of it. And then the white men rushed forward to peer down two hundred feet where they could see some shapeless lump lying still on the lower slope.

Only the crows kept going over with their lost cries. And the men, purged now and gazing emptily at the boulders and the dead, knew that no arrests would be made as the blacks, their faces drilled into nothing, stood motionless in this shock of tragedy.

Mr Boyd, rounding the base from the north and fighting clear of the straggly trees, saw a body hurtle from the cliff-top to the lower slope before the scarp. At first he thought it was some strange bird diving on prey, and he cantered his horse along easily to the spot where he discovered it was the prey itself he was looking at.

"My God," he breathed.

He dismounted and walked closer to bend over the crushed figure with its limbs stuck out at four grotesque angles. The skull had burst open and the rocks about were spattered with blood-flecked grey. And then, heaving at this, he saw the small body rolled to one side, howling at the end of a lifeless hand. His mind informed him it couldn't be as he bent over the unharmed child. Yet it was so. A miracle of salvation.

He picked it up and cradled it while it wailed thinly. It was naked save for a silver piece strung round its neck. The noon sun struck off the metal in small brilliant flashes and Boyd read Dorahy's name and puzzled. Puzzled for minutes, it seemed, when he became aware of figures at the top of the cliff looking down also and heard the rattle of hooves coming up behind him.

The three horsemen reined in. Dorahy's face was set in its usual sour and gentle lines, but there was an underlying tension of excitement. Jenner and his boy had an angry kind of bafflement about them.

They dismounted and joined him. Without words. The heat of the sun was full of speech. The baby wailed again as Dorahy came closer to examine the dead woman, the sadness of it, and then to look upward where the posse was outlined against searing cobalt.

Young Jenner, whose voice was choking, said something the others could not quite hear, but Dorahy spoke loudly for the boy and for all of them, his eyes fixed on the familiar and now disfigured body of the young woman.

"Lucretia," he said. "Lucretia lying naked."

BARNEY SWEETMAN is still the host of lush broad acres. He had owned most of the mill that crushed not only his cane crops but those of neighbouring farms. He had believed earnestly in Separation. He had implemented the policy of cheap black labour and in his minor hey-day had a barracks with thirty kanaka boys, the wide-veranda'd plantation house where he squired it around in white moleskins and blue oxford shirts. He had held many gracious drunken evenings on behalf of the Separation League for other planters in the district. Dorahy still recalls the night he had been invited for some crushing-season shenanigans, and on going to farewell his hosts had found the husband sprawled in the garden and the wife collapsed in the breeze-way. Tempted to recite a suitable fragment of Horace over their recumbent forms, he had been accosted by Snoggers Boyd who was still some drinks this side of sanity.

Dorahy has a sense of *déjà vu*. It is happening again as he edges towards the front door.

Snoggers says, "Not leaving are you? Don't leave. Spoil everything."

"I have to be sober to face tomorrow," Dorahy answers. At that other time he had added grimly, "I'm answerable to their sons."

Boyd had thought about this with some amusement patched at the corners of his mouth.

"But the parents aren't. To their sons, I mean. It's a strange world when outsiders have to set a better face on things." Now he says, "If you're leaving I can give you a lift."

"Well, perhaps," Dorahy says. "I wanted a chance to talk with you."

"Good," Boyd says. "I came with Buckmaster, but he seems to have passed out with jollity. Someone will get him home."

They look back in at the turmoil of upright but drink-flogged bodies. Buckmaster is snoring deeply from an easy chair.

"Yes," Boyd says sardonically. "Ah, yes."

They go back down the long hall and out onto the steps. The garden is sickly with frangipani and the overriding sweetness of cane. "In this small cloister," Dorahy wonders, "what vows are shattered daily?" And he asks abruptly, "Can you take me to Lunt?"

The crudity of the request startles Boyd.

"Well, now!" he says. There is a waiting pause. "When?"

"Tomorrow. At least as soon as possible. I have only the week."

"Why?"

"I think he should be here. For the official welcome."

"Why?"

"It pleases my sense of irony, I suppose. You think so, too."

"Do I? I don't know that I do. He'd probably refuse. It's twenty years, you know. Twenty."

They walk across to the side of the garden where Boyd's buggy is hitched to the fence. Despite the darkness, Boyd pauses before he puts one foot on the step and stares at the other man.

"Why won't you let go?" he asks.

"I can't," Dorahy says. "It's simply that I can't."

The ride back to the hotel is silent. But there is all the hushing surge of sea along the front. The streets, the disposition of them, haven't really changed; and consequently in the formless dark Dorahy feels tears prickling and taking shape behind his lids, so that when he gets out in front of the hotel with its sea-facing verandas and the long star-wash of the sky, he feels the merging of time then and time now.

"You don't really care for Lunt," Boyd accuses him over the handshake. "You're not a seeker after justice. You're just a trouble-maker." But he smiles.

"Perhaps you're right," Dorahy concedes. He feels unexpectedly humble. He is surprised into a silent admission of hatred greater than charity.

"You poor muddled bastard," Boyd says. "All right. I'll run you up there. My reasons are different. But I'll run you up. No persuasion though."

"What do you mean?"

"No trying to talk the old boy into coming if he doesn't want it. I'm very fond—or I used to be—of the old Charlie Lunt."

71

Dorahy leans against the buggy side a moment. He finds it hard to believe it has been so easy.

"Lunt's the only reason I came back," he says. And he is speaking the truth though it is a different truth for Boyd. "The only reason."

Boyd raises one hand before he takes the reins and shakes them. It is blessing and absolution in one.

ON THE veranda, post-breakfast, of the Sea Rip Hotel, Gracie Tilburn, still with magnificent voice, is holding forth. She has gathered her band of acolytes from fried eggs and bacon and a couple of anaemic cereals only. The veranda, open to morning sun with its striped deck-chairs and rachitic tables, is booming with reminiscence and gossip. Gracie had married twice and on neither occasion did her voice achieve the rich black quality she had been told came with sexual fulfilment. Still, it is rich enough. Her husbands' importance had petered away in direct ratio to her encores. Manless, she realises how much she had needed each of them.

Her busy brown eyes take in the group: Benjy Wilson, widower; old Miss Charlton who had run Sunday-school classes she had tried to avoid—she is very old now and nods agreement to everything; Ted Ellis and his wife, ex-groceries; Roy Armitage and Jack Romney, both wifeless but still grubbing for money on a shared mixed dairy farm down south. She smiles and it is radiant. The others could believe her to be about to burst into song—which no one will prevent, at least on the evening when the official speeches and welcomes have been made.

There are other groups scattered in chairs along the veranda, but they are younger or much older and have different references. Nostalgia has not united them all except in the accidents of greeting— the casual wave, the nod, the cursory handshake.

"I'm cramming this in between engagements," Gracie is confessing, "in Melbourne and Sydney. Simply squeezing it in. I very nearly couldn't come."

They are all grateful. Some even say so. It wouldn't have been the same.

"But where *is* everybody?" she is asking the sea and the palms along the front. "Where's Tim Jenner? Where's Freddie Buckmaster?"

Her rhetoric does not really need an answer, but she gets it from Ted Ellis.

"They'll be in later," Ellis says. He thinks slowly, speaks slowly. "I've been back before. Seen them. The Jenners still have the same holding, only the boy does most of the work now. Not a boy. Middle-aged man. And Freddie Buckmaster is down from the Palmer."

Gracie Tilburn is all ears. "They were dear boys," she says graciously. "Dear, dear boys. I wonder will I know them?" To a chorus of assent, she sips her tea.

Dorahy is espied slipping by to have a walk along the front so that Gracie, who uses her tongue with the ease of a tapir, uncoils a sentence in his direction that sucks him back. Her face hasn't really begun to crumble yet and Dorahy, pulling up another chair, is wedged in between pure art and Old Testament.

"Isn't it wonderful, Mr Dorahy," old Miss Charlton croaks, "to be back?"

Dorahy would want to harp on his obsession, but their morning faces are too bland.

"As if we'd never been away," Benjy Wilson says. "The town's hardly altered except for the size. Shops in the same old places. Same people." He has another go at lighting his pipe.

"How's the family now?" Dorahy asks him, playing conventional visitors.

"Well, the kids are all grown up. Don't need me any more. They've moved out and away."

"What about that youngest girl of yours? The one who was lost that time. What's she doing?"

Benjy suspects no reference to the darkness of the past. "She's made me a grand-dad three times over. In Brissy now, happily married and all."

"That's good," Dorahy says musingly. He thinks of Kowaha. "That's good. I don't suppose . . . oh, nothing!" He cannot proceed with what chokes him.

"Suppose what?" Wilson is a big lumbering man, still primitive and slowly suspicious despite grandfatherdom. Or because of it.

"Nothing," Dorahy says. "I was just remembering."

A hundred feet away reef waters lick at the sand strip. The heat comes fiercely to life as the sun moves in square blocks along the hotel terrace, painting in yellow spaces the colonnades of wrought-iron stanchion. They are all seated in sun now. Nothing can be hidden.

Gracie Tilburn for one cannot hide. She presses Dorahy with questions. Has he heard from Tim Jenner in all these years?

A card or two. A longish letter one Christmas, so long ago now he forgets the substance.

He says, "Not really," and the sun clouts the side of his head for the lie.

Gracie is thinking at half her age level, smoothing the silk over fatter thighs, recalling lazy-daisied hats and the grass of a lost creek. Grief keeps pecking at her for the vanished past when even her voice had seemed purer. Sentimental, she senses tears washing behind her eyes and quickly sips more tea.

But Argus-eyed Dorahy has observed. He puts a hand over hers as she reaches out for the sugar.

He says, "It's the same for all of us you know. Just the same."

And then he remembers the swollen face of young Jenner entering the world of men, and the sun loses some of its sting. Dubiety about his role of avenging prophet nibbles, but there is not sufficient bite for him to alter his determination.

Ted Ellis, with unforced bonhomie, says, "Soon be time for that first drink of the day," and gets Romney and Armitage on side in a flash, rum being thicker than blood.

"Why don't I have that gift?" Dorahy asks himself. He has planned a solitary mooch along the front to bathe in a world of water and light. He is not and never will be a man among men, while Romney is saying meanwhile that it can never be too early and Armitage heads for the bar to fetch and carry.

He decides to drink with them, get on side. Buckmaster, he knows, would have no trouble achieving a nexus. "I must try to be," he decides, rejecting the idea even as he does so, "more like Buckmaster." But it is too late for his crabby morality, and when the rum comes he can only sip in silence.

Affronted, Miss Charlton recalls something she has to do in her room; Ted Ellis's wife does the same; but Gracie Tilburn, who is used to being a woman among men, stays put and orders a teeny piece of brandy.

"Not enough to ruin the voice," she explains, and her explanation is so coy Dorahy flinches.

He asks the others in a kind of cold rage, then, about Charlie Lunt. The other men make weak feints at vagueness and memory until Dorahy catches Romney grinning at Armitage, a rictus of prior and secret knowledge.

"He's doing all right," Romney says. "Very all right."

Romney is an ursine fellow, still tough at fifty, and nobody's subaltern. When Gracie asks what he means by "very" he gives another grin to his stooge and says it isn't for ladies.

"Are you a lady?" he asks insolently.

Gracie takes it well. Time has given her a wonderful callus. She says she hopes she is, but the insult has stopped her momentarily, for she takes refuge in brandy while her eyes beg Dorahy's like a dog.

"Will Mr Lunt be coming?" she asks them, ladylike.

"Now that," Romney says with a laugh, "I seriously doubt."

Dorahy loathes the manner of the man. "I intend doing something about that. He should be here. An integral part of the place."

"And what are you going to do?" Armitage challenges. He is a blond, devious man. "He wasn't invited."

A conspiracy, Dorahy thinks. He says, "As my guest. He can come as my guest."

"But he's close enough to have come back before this if he'd wanted to. He hasn't set foot in the town since the day he left."

"And when was that?"

"Close on eighteen years now. Just after you'd gone."

Only Lunt remembers the force of the wind that day, wind driving apocalyptically across his dusty paddocks for grass scourings. The sulky had groaned under his few belongings, for he had sold out at a pittance, hardly enough to buy the mixed business he took over. He said good-bye to no one except the Jenners and whipped his horse up for the trip north.

"Poor old devil!" Dorahy complains. "He was forced out. He had no option."

"Fair go!" Romney says, quietly warning. "You can leave us out of it."

But the other man pursues. "Were you not," he nags pedantically,

76

"part of the punitive force in those days, sidekicks to young Buck-master?"

"Where you should have been," Armitage answers flatly. "Christ! You're not going to muck-rake like this!" He slams his glass down in a mess of slop and spill. "We haven't come back to go chewing over the past."

"I thought that was why we had come."

"Witty bastard, eh?"

Gracie Tilburn is finally offended by this manifestation of maleness. She rises despite Dorahy's "Don't go."

The other three men are not even aware. Ted Ellis keeps grinning stupidly, but silk sweeps off and a lingering perfume plagues these perimeters of violence.

"We all have to dig dirt and eat dirt," Dorahy counters. He is sick at heart with their reactions but feels doomed to thrust and thrust at the matter even until someone might quieten him with a blow. "People should face up to what they have done. I only want repentance. For his sake. He was a good man."

Romney swallows the remainder of his drink in a huge gulp that hurts the muscles of his throat. Everything about him is powerful, even his steady and obtuse refusals that drive Dorahy into more prob-ing.

Dorahy keeps flicking the sore place until one of them tells him to shut up about Lunt and, manly, buys him a second pacifier rum. He drinks it gloomily, watching the few foolish swimmers who have appeared on the beach.

DORAHY IS fretting along the water-front on the second day, trying out the equation between blue water and blue air while he waits for Boyd. Words plague his mind. It is all words in angry buzzing debate, the most boneless of arguments, that sees no end of relief. He is sick with them, maddened by the circularity of theme that leaves him standing where he had begun. And it is on this point of noon hopelessness that Boyd's clopping buggy noses him out as he shelters below a tattered palm.

"Against my better judgment," Boyd says, leaning over the side. "Get in."

They sit in silence for a few moments while the horse snorts at flies. Dorahy removes his panama and flicks back the wet hair.

"I was despairing," he offers.

"A man must be mad," Boyd agrees. "But I'm keeping my word. My half-promise, that is."

Dorahy regards the sweating horse wonderingly.

"How far, then, is it?"

"Not far. About thirty. If we take it easy we'll make it by tea-time. She's pretty fresh."

"So he's as close as that! Well!" It is anti-climactic after all.

"Close enough for what you're trying to do," Boyd says. "But we'll have to stop the night to rest the horse. It could be quite pleasant— little fishing village north-east of The Leap." He looks hard at Dorahy. "You're sure you still want to go? You know what you're doing?"

"Quite sure." He looks at Boyd in return. Perhaps the maggot will stop gnawing when . . . "It's very good of you," he says.

"It is," Boyd agrees. "Something tells me it is the wrong thing."

He gives the reins a shake and the buggy pulls out smartly on the dirt road.

Jogging between the cane-field hedges from which heat and sweetness pour out, Dorahy confronts his demon with the pacifics of landscape, absorbing the scattered farmhouses, the kids waving from fence perches. He refuses to see himself as a trouble-maker. Wasn't that what Boyd had suggested? Already, in his dedication to seek reprisal or justice, he has involved himself so thoroughly in the politics of this small town it could be as if he had never left. When the cane-fields give out to the scrubbier landscape that looks as if it has only been pencilled in, the satisfaction of alienation comes back to him.

"This is good of you," Dorahy says once more, glancing at Boyd's stubby profile.

"We've agreed on that. But I'm still not sure why I—or even you, for that matter—am doing it."

"You're doing it for the same reason as me, I suppose. Or rather, I suspect."

"We'll see," Boyd answers.

He has slowed the horse down to a walk. The flies keep pestering beneath the brims of their hats. Dust puffs and filters and becomes a small cloud behind them. The last farmhouse has been left behind and the loneliness of trees reaches in to them on the narrow road. In the sultry air Dorahy finds himself nodding. Once or twice he jerks awake when Boyd flicks the horse into a trot and is aware of the other man sucking stolidly at his pipe, his face set like a compass needle on the twisting road ahead.

An hour trudges by. Mandarana looms up, its great hulk black on their right. Both men look and then ignore. Their thoughts are twinned for the moment and they each see the Sunday landscape, the body, the men on the peak.

"It's just past here, the turn-off," Boyd says. "There's a bit of a creek in a mile or so. I think we'll stop a while and give the old girl a breather. The road gets pretty rough after this. It's not much more than a track."

Boyd is strangely regretful now he has come so far, and he takes his eyes off the rutty road for a minute to inspect the map of Dorahy's face. The sour gentleness is implacable. "God help him," he prays humorously to himself. "He's obsessed and I am yielding to his vice." He guides the horse steadily and pessimistically on, but she is more skilled than he and picks her own way delicately between pot-holes. The road gives its own mandates.

On a grassy spit of the creek Boyd unharnesses the horse, hobbles her, and lets her crop the feed along the bank. The two men stretch out beneath a tree, smoking quietly, trying out their obsessions in silence. Above, the sky has become sulky with a huge boil-up of cloud from the sea, heavy cumulus dark with rain on its underside. Even in the hollow they are aware of a freshening in the air as small pre-storm winds rattle the trees.

"I'll make a cuppa," Boyd says. He fetches a billy and tea from the back of the buggy and in a few minutes has a small fire blazing between rocks by the water.

"How far now?" Dorahy asks. He is beginning to feel the mendicant.

"About the same distance again," Boyd says. He hands Dorahy a tin mug, fills his own from the billy, and sips, speculating on obsession and the places it takes one. "There are a couple of big cane farms out this way, two of the biggest in the district. I suppose old Charlie makes out with that and the few old fisherboys who live in his village. He never wanted much. Just to be let alone, I think."

"And I'm not doing that!" Dorahy sounds resentful.

"You said it," Boyd answers with a laugh. "I'm merely the guide."

Warm rain-splash falls on them suddenly. The fire hisses between the rocks.

"That's it!" Boyd says, looking up at the sky. "I'd better harness up or we'll get soaked."

Carefully he douses the fire with sand and, genial about Dorahy's uselessness, hitches his horse back between the shafts, and guides the buggy up the slope onto the track.

"Old girl!" he exclaims in sudden affection, slapping her fat rump, and momentarily preferring her to his bedevilled passenger. He hauls up the buggy hood and takes his seat, still clutching his unfinished mug of tea. Dorahy climbs in beside him, and the rain, bursting above them, drums hard on the canvas and bounces off the buggy steps.

"Shall we sit it out or go?" Boyd asks.

"Go," Dorahy replies. He is alive with fever, a spiritual temperature that flushes only the soul. He could be shaking, but he ignores this, setting his eyes on the last leg of the journey like a frantic pilgrim.

The horse is frisky after her rest, but the track, cutting through mountain country to the sea, argues every foot of the way. It is not until they have come through the worst of it and the ruts widen into a dusty road leading to the east that the horse can sharpen into a trot, bowling them briskly into ploughed country black under the rain. Sheds stand on sky-lines. Three paddocks away a shuttered farmhouse turns its back. Three more hills and they can glimpse the sea below and to the north and east of them. Dorahy shifts restlessly on his seat. But it is another half-hour before the buggy rolls onto the wide sea-gazing clearing with its half-dozen shacks and the shanty of a store they have come to find.

In the easing rain, Boyd hitches his horse to the storepost and waits for Dorahy, who is sensing the full purpose of the journey at this moment, not merely the country ride they have come, and now the grey spread of sea. Boyd leads the way into the store, brushing heavily against the sacking drape that is hauled roughly to one side, and, in that inner twilight against which they can hear the steady comment of reef waters, rings a small handbell on the counter.

From the back of the shop there is a sound—cough? cry?—and someone is heard walking through.

Dorahy has his mouth ready to smile—the crisis of the dream—but it is a young woman who appears, a full-blood with crisp hair and a deeply pigmented skin. She looks at the two men standing there in front of the tinned goods, the grocery packets, puzzles for a moment, and then smiles at Boyd.

"Remember me, Mary?" he asks. "Willie Boyd. How are you?" Amusedly he catches onto Dorahy's surprised eyes. "This is Kowaha's little girl," he explains. "Grown up."

In this lost settlement washed up by the sea, the introductions are a banal joke.

"This is Mr Dorahy who knew you years ago."

But Dorahy is back at Mandarana's foot gazing down at the shattered body, the outrage of it, the baby in Boyd's arms. Something like tears is threatening. He cannot speak, only smile and stiffly take her hand into his. Shyly she draws back.

"Charlie around?" Boyd asks. "Tell him there's a couple of friends."

She smiles again, turning to go softly through the rear door of the shop and into the house. Within the minute they can hear his clumping irregular footsteps coming through.

Lunt has grown older. The seams on his face match those in Dorahy's soul as he takes Lunt's hand. Boyd watches them both curiously and sighs for the matter of it. But Lunt is full of astonishment.

"The surprise of it!" he keeps saying. "What a day! The surprise of it!" He is all smiles. "Come through," he invites them, opening the flap in the counter for them. "Come through."

His parlour is tiny. There are two chairs, a small table and some books. The room is jammed already. A small window looks out on a shaggy yard with a lemon-tree. "If this is the last-post nest," Dorahy thinks with pity—which is misplaced—"then the man is caged."

He wants to open something to let him out and it seems a pedantic shame merely to be going through how-are-you motions when inside him there is a voice shouting, "Remember when—?"

Lunt is slower, too; yet there is a deliberateness about him signalled by his face that has been hewn into a mask of forgiveness and tolerance despite those small lines of withdrawal. He says, Yes he had heard of the Back to The Taws week, and No he had not received any letter or invitation. Which amuses him. He supposes he could have gone up had he wanted. He laughs creakingly and listens with a smile to the simplicity of Dorahy's invitation while Boyd frowns with annoyance.

"Well, I was waiting to be asked," he admits. "But you don't want me back to please me," he accuses shrewdly. "Only to please yourself."

Boyd has to laugh with relief. "That's exactly what I say, Charlie. Don't listen to him."

Dorahy feels ashamed. But it is a temporary shame. He is mounted and away.

"It's justice I want done."

"You want exposure," Lunt says bluntly. "Fancy, after all this time!" He marvels at it. "I've grown like an oyster onto this bit of reef," he says, and looks past them at the backyard, needing no other solace. "Still," he adds, "it's nice to be asked—even for the wrong reasons. Very nice. I thought I'd been forgotten."

"Not that," says Boyd, who is guilty of neglect.

"That young woman," Lunt says looking at Dorahy. "Mary. Boyd's probably told you she's Kowaha's child. It's a long story. I won't bother you with it. But she came to me quite voluntarily about six years ago and asked if she could look after me. The Jenners had her till then. But I suppose you know all this. What I wanted to tell

82

you"—he smiles at the memory—"she still has that medal you gave her. Dorahy's luck. Remember?"

Dorahy remembers. He can only nod.

"No," Lunt goes on. "No. Not what you're thinking. She helps in the shop and cooks for me, but that's all. She has a husband now. Works on the cane." He thinks of the girl, years ago, who had never, not ever—and his face saddens.

Dorahy is silent. Something tells him he will win by waiting.

"Look," Lunt says and he chuckles, "I might come if I could bring her, too. That would make them sit up."

"They'd use her to rip you apart," Boyd warns. "They'd say you're a gin lover and grind your face in it."

"It has been ground before," Lunt says simply.

"Think about it," Dorahy pleads, sensing a weakening.

Lunt only smiles. "You two," he says, "you're not going back to-night. We'll have a yarn, eh? I can make you shakedowns on the veranda and we'll have a bite to eat. It's been a long time."

Boyd grimaces as if the pain has been transferred to him.

"We'd love to stay," he says. "Ignore this mad bastard who has his axe to grind. We've come to see you."

Lunt looks thoughtful. "It's nice to have been asked, anyway," he repeats. "Oh, I wouldn't be coming to please Tom. Just myself. Maybe a change away from here would do me good. I've only been away once in the last eighteen years. A man rots a bit."

Dorahy decides to press home. "Then you may come?" He is greedy as a child.

"Oh, my God, Tom," Boyd groans. "Leave it."

"We'll see," Lunt says. "I'll sleep on it."

Boyd sighs and shrugs. Is there some especial charisma in Dorahy, some magnetic tug that draws others like filings? Why, there's enough of the irritant in the fellow, he knows, to alienate people by scores. He understands this and yet still sees himself the willing courier drawn by some particular ascetic quality in the man. Fanaticism always has its disciples, he thinks bitterly. But why me?

THE SCHOOL OF ARTS is jammed with protestations of loyalty.

Someone has tacked bunting round the stage where a table and chairs have been set up for the welcoming committee. The whole room has a faded and worn-out look, but no one's complaining.

There are three hours yet before the committee begins its self-adulatory session of whoopee.

And perhaps three hours are enough for Buckmaster, who has heard of Dorahy's proposal to bring Lunt up for the opening hoo-ha. He rages inwardly and silently, a rage all the worse for its containment, and goes to Sweetman's house where he will renew his anger.

Sweetman's calm refuels Buckmaster.

"It won't matter," he says. "There's nothing now that can be done. They can stir up the past a little, I suppose, but everyone here will be beyond it. We're beyond it."

They are pacing about the front garden, monks of misrule, amid the sterile ambience of scentless gorgeous tropicana. The sky is crazy with stars.

"He must be stopped," mad Buckmaster says. "When are they due back?"

"Benjy Wilson says they set off up the coast some time yesterday. They should be back soon—if they're coming."

"Then we'll have to intercept them."

Sweetman snaps off an allamanda bloom and examines it so minutely he might be seeking his salvation in the flower's golden centre. Buckmaster's clenched fists whiten with the effort not to dash it from him—salvation and flower.

84

"My boy says to count him in," he continues. "He's willing to do something."

"What?"

Buckmaster lets the question pass. He'd let a lot of questions pass in his day, politically practising.

"Can I count on you?" he asks suddenly.

Sweetman worries this one. "To do anything now," he says, "might be a lot worse than simply letting him come, celebrate, if that's what he's here for, and go away again. In any case he might have refused. Tom Dorahy can't force him to come."

"But it's not Lunt I'm worried about," Buckmaster says. "It's that bloody schoolteacher. He always was a great nose-shover into other people's affairs."

"A stinking, righteous man," Sweetman says with a smile. "You hate them, don't you? Well, maybe Boyd's horse will lame or an axle break. Then your problem will be solved. But count me out of your plans. Do what you like. Only be warned, Jim, don't mess up things for the rest of us."

Yet Boyd's buggy is immune to bone-pointing. It comes back into town an hour after sunset and in the deeper dark takes Dorahy and Lunt home to Boyd's. And it is then, as they drag cramped limbs down and move into the shadow of trees, that Dorahy receives the first shattering blow and Lunt the second.

There is nothing Boyd can do: there is only the sound of the attackers' horses cantering away. He shouts for his wife and proceeds to lug Dorahy over to the steps. Then his wife appears and bends over Lunt, who has managed to sit up. Her stooped figure contains elements of tribal lament.

Dorahy comes to slowly. His head is an enormous throbbing pain which he holds in both hands.

"Well," Boyd says, unable to keep the satisfaction of being right from his voice, "that's the first of it. Don't say you weren't warned. A taste of stay-off, I wouldn't be surprised. Do you still want to go to the welcome-in?"

Boyd's wife has come down into the dewy garden with a bowl of water and bits of rag with which she is making wet plasters. She moves from Lunt to Dorahy, bathing and murmuring. At fifty the beauty of her bones is even more apparent, and the tenderness she has always

85

felt for Lunt springs like an act of contrition in the movements of tending. She recalls him as he was twenty years ago and is surprised how the moral rigidities of that time have moulded themselves into deeper statements.

"Of course they will be going," she says. "Especially because of this."

Seated in their living-room, the whirring in the skull subsiding: "Dearest Lucy," Dorahy muses, "have I ever argued with you yet?"

He watches her setting the table, serving dinner, and he absorbs the gentleness of her hands. He knows why he had never married before, that other time, and seeing her now reaffirms his reasons. The fire within her is rarely suspected by those who see only the skin of another, but Dorahy had years ago caught glimpses of flame that alone served to underscore her perfection for him.

"We'll be going," he says. "The four of us."

Boyd winces.

"What sort of confrontation are you after?" he demands. "Words or silence? Violence, is it? Something of what they have just done to you? Will you make a public accusation? It would harm you more, and you know it. Their tricky lawyers would see to that."

"I'm going to blast a way through the Alps with vinegar," he says. And then he laughs.

The protective warmth of the Boyds has an amniotic quality. Pain subsides. His soul is more swollen than the tenderness above his right eye; and amazement that the same bullish tactics are in vogue over-whelms him.

He eases himself upright on the sofa and, leaning over towards Lunt, says, "I brought this on you. I'm sorry." He is a man who finds it difficult to apologise. Squirming a way out, he berates himself, with the moist eye, the propitiatory throb in the voice! The insincerity of it! He cannot tolerate this self-revulsion, though it is a thing he feels more often as he grows older.

Lunt says, "I won't be turned into a martyr against my will. But the bastards have roused me this time. I'll go into that pompous ballyhoo with this whacking great headache and show I won't be forced out."

Boyd is pouring rums and there is immediate solace.

"This will cut through more than the Alps," he says.

86

And he is right, after all, Dorahy recognises, as the bite of it melts the inner rage.


Snoggers Boyd, entering into the spirit of it at last, has pinned sarcastic pieces of bunting, tie-shaped, to their collars. Lunt enjoys, but Dorahy merely tolerates. They make a pretty picture, he thinks, posed here preparatory to entering the old School of Arts from whose pediment sad streamers hang in reply.

People are moving up from either side, blocking the stairs as they revive memories in passageways too narrow for them or their inflated nostalgia. One quick glance and there, just inside the doorway, is Buckmaster shaking hands with visitors in an air loud with greetings and cries of recognition. The hall is too voluble.

While they pause before the crowd, a red-haired fellow with a wide smile comes up to Dorahy.

"How are you, sir?" he asks slipping automatically into the language pattern of his school days, and equally familiarly Dorahy slips back twenty years and says, "Well, thank you, young Jenner." They both laugh.

Time, thinks Dorahy, time! How it has gouged out the tenderness of youth, though there is still much that is innocent about the youngish man before him—the steadiness of eye, the firmness of mouth.

"I've come," Tim Jenner confesses, "to pave the way through Scylla and Charybdis. Barney Sweetman's up there, too. The wandering rocks. I'll release my father and we'll sail through in his wake."

Dorahy notices then the elderly man behind him. For the first flashing second he does not think "There go I" but "How he has aged!" Then he realises he is looking at a twin scarring of time. The paint has run on the masks, trickles that make the facsimile sour or disillusioned. Old Jenner looks frail now, but then so does Dorahy.

"Good to see you, Tom," old Jenner says. "And you, Charlie. What a marvellous surprise!" He takes both of Lunt's hands and holds them warmly. "Wonderful to have you here with us—for whatever we're celebrating. Maybe because we are at last a fading point on the map."

He is partly right, for the town has steadily drained out its people for ten years since the boom. There is no talk of Separation Leagues now, though this evening has brought about a quorum. Dorahy's head still throbs and he is giddy with yap and lights. He notices Lunt pass his hand wearily across his eyes and asks how he feels.

"Pretty terrible," Lunt replies. "I'm beginning to feel sorry I came. There seems to be some sort of brigade at the top of the stairs, too. Do you think they'll let us in?"

"We'll see," Dorahy says. "We'll see. I wish I wasn't feeling so foul."

Their party moves towards the congestion at the foot of the stairs where Gracie Tilburn is holding preliminary court. Momentarily Dorahy closes his eyes, reasoning falsely that she won't see him. He hopes blindness makes him invisible for the pounce, which comes, on the moment, with a richly pitched cry. She demands his recognition but her eyes are on Tim Jenner whose hands she seizes with palpable ardour. She is magnificent in puce, through the pink waves of which young Jenner is struggling towards a dream of pallid blue and lazy daisies. He cannot accept her at once, though her hands are demanding on his own.

He says, "Why, Gracie! Gracie!" but his voice is limp.

"When I sing," Gracie tells herself, "oh, when I sing it will be different."

She is not so unsubtle that she cannot notice his hesitancy; but bravely the slim girl, who is still present inside this plump woman, greets Boyd's little group with kisses all round, cheek after cheek. The grand gesture. "There," she reasons crazily, "I have put my mark on them." To her this means possession. Consequently she is all graciousness when they reach the small lobby in which Buckmaster and Sweetman are waiting.

They are overcome by puce.

Even their words, "I'm afraid this gentleman cannot—", are confused and drowned as she sweeps by. But they still bail Lunt up.

"Where's your invitation?" Buckmaster demands.

Lunt, still groggy from the head blow, looks up, recognises, and is silent.

"I'm afraid this won't do," Sweetman says, coming across. "It won't really do at all. We're sorry."

Jenner and Boyd shove their faces into the group.

"Nonsense," Snoggers says. "Of course it will do. They're all my guests."

Newcomers are impatient behind them.

88

"Would you mind standing to one side?" Sweetman asks. "Just till we get things sorted out. It won't take long."

"Bloody nonsense!" Dorahy cries. "We're going in."

The scuffle as Buckmaster and Sweetman converge on him and Lunt is a blunt parrying of arms at which more newcomers stare in delighted puzzlement. Buckmaster is almost bursting with the effort not to punch.

"Come along, come along!" Boyd says, edging his wife forward. And more softly, "You can't afford to be seen like this. It won't go well with the voters."

A minion is tapping Buckmaster's arm. It is almost time for the officials to go up on stage.

"God bugger you," Buckmaster whispers to Dorahy. "Get in then. Get bloody in before I kill you."

The hall is packed. As Dorahy fumbles his way along a row towards a group of empty chairs at the side, he is again amazed at the familiarity of faces like maps of countries he has once visited. The contours have subtly changed. The rivers have altered their flow. Hills are steeper. Yet they hold sufficient of their early selves to make recognition possible in the way one says, "And there was the corner store. There the newsagent. Once I ran along here where a hedge used to be." He takes his place beside Lunt who is managing his wooden leg awkwardly and observes Gracie Tilburn a row away twisting to catch his eye.

Gracie waves. She will be singing shortly and has no doubts about her magic. Like an empress, her bounds are infinite, and when Barney Sweetman spots her (he has glimpsed the wave) and invites her to join the official party, she concurs with statuesque magnificence.

Up here on stage, she decides, seated near the jug and the water glasses, is my true home. There are no corner stores in Gracie's vision, no newsagent with dog-stained hoardings, no hedges. There is only the blurred flow of faces and the noise made by hands.

A large lady arranges her behind at the piano. The queen is saved in a series of mundane chords. Everyone is standing for these moments, and when the anthem finishes Sweetman steps forward and waits like an old stager for all to be seated and all sound to subside. He's used to this, anyone can see, catching with his eye every trout in the stream.

"Dear old friends," he begins (and that's a smasher), "for I know I can call all of you that, on looking around this hall I am amazed and touched—yes, touched—by the number of people who have responded to my invitation to come home. For this is home for many of us still and was home once for those of you who have gone away to make your lives elsewhere. But even to them I say this is *still* home, the place in which you took first steps to manhood, uttered your first meaningful words, made your first plans, indulged your first dreams."

He pauses, having gauged the response to a nicety, as the applause breaks out.

"For many of you, rather I think for each and every one of you"—"Two," Dorahy murmurs to himself counting clichés—"those dreams were fulfilled. The point is that the memories and experiences you formulated here twenty years ago are still part of you and what you have become—part of this town. And the people who were in it when you were in it have become part of your blood."

"Hear hear!" shouts derisive Dorahy who is losing control.

People turn to stare and smile. But it doesn't rattle Sweetman.

"Now this is a good thing," he continues, not stalling for a moment, "for the town owes all of you something and all of you are indebted to the town. It is a marriage of place and person that cannot be ignored."

Strategy pause. The people watching him are subdued. This is not a moment for clapping. It is a tender moment made for silence, for seriousness. They all ache for his next words.

"Before I go further I have on stage with me someone who needs no introduction"—"Three," counts Dorahy—"to any of you. I refer of course to our own Miss Gracie Tilburn who has come all the way back from the south to be with us on this happy occasion." ("Four," he counts.) "She has graciously consented to sing for us once more, and those of you who remember her singing from twenty years back will know that is something for which we are indebted. It is moving to think that at the height of her fame and the peak of her career"—"Oh, my God!" says Dorahy, who has lost count—"she chooses to return here, to her birth-place, to sing for us. Ladies and gentlemen, I give you Miss Gracie Tilburn."

The racket of applause. Gracie stands modestly during it, and now moves over to the piano where the pianist is shuffling sheets of music. The opening notes of "Home, Sweet Home" are played and then Gracie, with ever so little trace of a throb, begins to sing. Her voice is richer, fuller, darker than in youth. The audience is emotionally stilled within its own darkness; but Dorahy whispers, "Say, eleven," so audibly his neighbours frown and shush him.

With an effort he constrains himself from leaping up and roaring, "It's nonsense! All nonsense!"

The applause is enormous at the end of the song. Hands are pulped. A huge and garish bouquet is rushed forward and Sweetman who is on his feet has taken the singer's hand. Smiles fly through the air like rockets.

Sweetman finally raises an arm for silence.

"Dear friends," he says again, "that response speaks for itself more than anything I can say. Thank you indeed, and thank you, Gracie—I may call you that?—for a wonderful opening of welcome. Those simple and unaffected words mean so much to us all. And now I'm going to call on James Buckmaster to say a few words. Ladies and gentlemen, James Buckmaster."

Tim Jenner has been affected. He is sixteen and gulping in great gobbets of Gracie's voice. He is down by the creek watching hat shadows alter the planes of her face. He is bashed outside the stock-and-station agent's. And he remembers the purity of his adolescent love with an ache that will not leave him free to hear Buckmaster's opening remarks. He only comes to during ". . . what we have done for this town is to build and strengthen it, to shape its future by the efforts of all who lived and worked here, some of us in small ways, perhaps; others in bigger ways—but all to the one purpose."

He pauses. Tim Jenner glances along the row at Dorahy, who is wrestling with an inner devil.

"This town has been built on sacrifice—self-sacrifice if you like—which is something that must take precedent when struggle and effort are required."

Suddenly Dorahy is on his feet shouting, "That's the word—sacrifice. How many? How many, eh, did you sacrifice?"

The hall is shocked. There are angry rumbles and two men come from the rear of the hall to seize the maniac by the arms. As they drag him out, he is still shouting, and when the porch is reached one of the bouncers whacks him hard across the side of the head.

"The world of men," he murmurs, looking up at his guards.

Boyd has forced his own way out to the porch. "Leave him," he says to the bouncers. "I'll get him home. He's not well. Come on, old chap," he says.

91

But Dorahy, dazed from this second blow, flaps like a bird, unable to stand. He argues pitifully, "I'm perfectly well. Get back in there. Get back in and show those sycophants!"

Boyd's hands and manner are firm. Somehow he steers him down the steps and across the road to where the buggy is hitched. The air is smelling of rain. "One blessing," thinks Boyd. Renewed hosannahs from the hall reach their ears and Dorahy frets again against Boyd's arms. "It's no use, Tom," Boyd says. "No use at all."

The hotel is like a shell cast up by the sea. Its only sound is the breathy echo of waves clamped against the listening ear. Boyd stumbles with him up the stairs and to his room, where Dorahy lies flopped on his bed and looks up vaguely.

"God!" is all he can say. "Oh, my God!"

Boyd uncaps a whisky flask. "Try this," he says. But it only strengthens Dorahy's tongue which lashes again and again, coiling like a whip round the same topic.

"I'll have to return soon," Boyd says at last. "Don't worry about Lunt. We'll put him up. Try to get some sleep."

Boyd is not a big man, but rising, finds himself towering over this rinsed-out fellow. Dorahy's cheek has swollen. The eye is already darkening.

L UNT IS NOT interested in retribution. He is a simple man and curious, with the inquisitiveness of the newly hatched. Yet there is no mischief in him.

After Dorahy has been hustled from the hall he continues sitting, stolidly listening to another three speeches, all kindred, and a final bracket of nostalgic songs from Gracie Tilburn. Ultimately the audience, an unintelligent monster, shoves its grotesque way to a room at the back of the hall where trestle tables support a sandwich supper. In the middle of this turmoil of recognition and reminiscence, the wave forming, breaking and petering out, the Jenners, Lucy Boyd and Lunt form a hard little knot which many of those present attempt to untie.

Sweetman pushes through the room to this boil lest it erupt. He cannot believe in the tolerance of others.

"Sorry we had to do that." He is referring to Dorahy. Old Jenner permits himself a smile while his son looks grave. "It could have been much worse. We have to think of the guests, the visitors. It's not pleasant to have someone going on like that at a reunion that should be friendly and warm. Not pleasant at all. We owe the others something."

Young Jenner says quietly, "A lot is owed to many people in this place."

"True. But we must live and let live."

"Especially with the elections coming up next month."

Sweetman replies with a poise that earns respect. "Right again. I won't pretend with you. When have I ever pretended? I feel I contribute something to the welfare of this place and I intend to go on contributing."

He is speaking more softly. All round them mouths are gobbling and gabbling. His back is slapped as he is hailed by wolfish passers and his smile of unutterable sweetness comes again and again between trivia utterances that for him have the utmost seriousness. He wears his geniality like a coat that he slips on and off with ease.

Tim Jenner is amused by such public-man antics and is still smiling at his own thoughts as Gracie Tilburn pushes to his side in the crush and slips an arm through his.

"Hullo," she carols. There is a faint whiff about her of lost summer days. Her face has plumped out and strengthened. "Remember?"

Too well, he thinks, twitching with the beginnings of a small pain that recaptures her voice and her throat, the sun-warmed hands of her by the creek. These subtleties are almost lost now as life has hardened the externals. He could weep for innocence, but says instead, "Of course. Your voice is still wonderful. Better, if anything."

"Tim," she says. "Oh, Tim." And she remembers one special day when she sang for him and Freddie Buckmaster in a summer-filled living-room and the voice, as if no longer part of her, made patterns like tapestry that she wove at exquisite will. Sad it is, thinks young middle-aged Jenner now, to hear that wistfulness from this stouter woman with a carapace of assurance. Losing as one grows. And the longing growing greater as one lives.

"I suppose you're married now?" she asks.

"Yes," he replies simply. "And you?"

"Was," she says. "Twice." And giggles like a girl. "The last is over now. Five years. A mistake."

Stagily she makes tiny mouths. Turns down the corners bravado style. Raises them. She is tempted to ask him if he is happy but senses his answer; and the heaviness of Sweetman's presence, and that of the father, the quiet confidence of Lucy Boyd—all oppress her. Deciding on gaiety, she tralas a little, asks after Fred Buckmaster and has him pointed out to her across the room. Her waves attract him.

"The gang's all here," Tim Jenner says. "God Almighty!" And Sweetman frowns at this and allows himself to be caught by another prodigal and drawn away.

Lunt is still chuckling as Freddie Buckmaster heaves his sweating bully-boy way towards them, stopping briefly every yard to pummel or shake other bully-boy paws.

"Well?" he asks, arriving on the tail-end of the chuckle and observing this limping stranger with an almost knowledge. "What's the joke, eh? Good night, isn't it? Wonderful night!" His enthusiasm is fake-right at this moment as he glares into Lunt's marvellously open eye. He shakes the firm hand of old Jenner, catches Gracie ("Gracie, I'd know you after a thousand years!") by the shoulders and gives her a smacking kiss on the cheek, says let bygones be bygones to young Jenner, and salutes his introduction to Lunt with the briefest nod. He is a practical man, and what cannot help him he refuses to acknowledge.

"How are you feeling, Mr Lunt?" he finally asks, driven by curiosity. "I heard you and Mr Dorahy had a spot of trouble earlier tonight."

"I'm getting too old for rough-house," Lunt says. "Does my presence alone incite?" He doesn't want an answer.

"We're a peaceable lot," Buckmaster says ambiguously. "We're not after trouble."

"Nor am I."

"It's not you. It's your mate. Why can't he keep his mouth shut, eh? What's he got to start stirring things up for?"

"We all have a destiny," Lunt says. He is feeling old and giddy and the stump of his leg throbs.

"Twaddle!" the ex-lieutenant says. "Where's Snoggers?"

"He's taken Mr Dorahy back to his hotel."

"Well, now, has he? What was the trouble? Too much grog?"

"Too much honesty," Lunt replies.

This sharp one goes home. A surly red shows on Fred Buckmaster's cheeks, exceeding the rouging that liquor and climate have given his skin. He says slowly, "I don't know about that."

On cue Boyd returns and sticks his head into the circle, one arm lightly slung about his wife's shoulders. He has a need to touch which no one has ever guessed at.

He says, "Know all about what?"

"Forget it!" Buckmaster says.

"You're not talking about old Tom Dorahy, are you? I've put him safely to bed feeling very frail." And continues thinking, "He's not the stuff of martyrs but of fanatics."

"I don't understand any of this," Gracie complains. Her coyness is being undermined by their intensity which she suspects but fails to digest. "Enough of this oblique talk! We're here to enjoy ourselves. Freddie, tell me all, I insist, all that's happened to you."

His confidences will liberate hers which are choking her in their urgency to be freed. Yet she plays the game and waits. Lucy Boyd has gone back for more tea. Someone is offering limp biscuits and sandwiches.

Freddie Buckmaster proffers the sort of information that he hopes will give him absolution. He tells her he has two boys. He tells her of the pub on the Palmer. And finally he swings on Lunt and asks him what he is doing back in the old place after all this time. Lunt regards him speculatively. Buckmaster is not a wise man, Lunt knows, and there is a brutality about him still that makes the older man cautious.

"Affection," he admits finally. "I liked the old place. I'm hoping for something. I don't know what. Now I'm getting on and feel gentler about things it seemed right to return. Just to see."

Freddie Buckmaster lets out a great guffaw, understanding nothing of what the old man has just said, but discovering some elusive effeminacy in the remarks.

"You must tell my old man that," he says between splutters. "You must tell my old man."

"He knows."

Young Buckmaster fails to understand this. He is obsessed with hard facts.

"But you only live thirty or so miles away. You could have come back before this. For affection!"

"No," Lunt says. "I was waiting to be asked. You see, I was driven out."

Right across the township people are yawning and dragging from beds. In the Sea Rip Hotel Freddie Buckmaster gives one final look at Gracie Tilburn, who is too bloody fat for his taste anyway, and heaves his own porky body into daytime.

As he dresses he marvels how he happened to get here. It was after the reception, he groggily recalls, and after the country women's supper, and after that his sulky to drive her home, a bit of spooning along the water-front—and then this. Well, he'd achieved it anyway after all these years. Beaten Tim Jenner to first base at last.

Gracie rolls heavily over and looks up. She feels all flesh. Her eyes widen vaguely as she looks at this man dragging on a tie four feet from her bed, and then she remembers. "Oh, my God," she thinks, and is filled with self-disgust. His gross thighs in shirt-tails appal. She wonders, if he obliterates them with trousers, whether she might be able to deny the whole thing.

"Darling," she lies, thinking of Tim Jenner, "what happened last night?"

He swings his coarse face on her and winks.

"Come off it," he says. "Come off it! We just had a bit of a get together." He finishes with his tie and proceeds to drag on his trousers.

Gracie thinks "Thank God" and smiles at him ravishingly. "I wish it hadn't been you," she tells herself. And she goes on smiling at him while thinking of Tim Jenner.

"Well," says this horror leaning over her, "I'll be toddling."

His reluctant kiss senses some of her own disgust.

"How long are you down for?" Gracie asks, feeling an insane need to make small talk.

"Just for the week," he replies, buttoning up. "The wife will hold the fort. She can hold anything. Great woman, that. Even toss out the drunks."

"Really!" Gracie yawns again and wishes he would go. "Then we'll see each other again. Maybe tomorrow."

"Count on that." He is lying also.

Closing the door behind him after blowing one last vulgar smacking kiss, he is jaunty as a dog let out. Almost he cocks one leg and makes such speed down the hotel staircase he misses the breakfast gong by seconds and is out on the front wrapped in innocuousness.

Gracie lies there and in a conglomerate of memories inspects husbands one and two. George becomes Frank in this melting process where she recalls George's blows and Frank's greed as one and the same thing. George had been handsome not only for her, and had finally sped absent-mindedly under a dray between one adultery and another. It still hurt to see him, even if only in the mind, alerting like a pointer at any woman who entered the room. But Frank she had simply left and almost forgotten. His monetary stinginess, his management of her funds had made it easy. He had lived off her voice like some huge parasite, and while she sang for both their suppers he had resigned from or lost one job after another, putting his idleness down to her need to have a manager. Gracie's mouth curls up in amusement at the thought of him on that last day when she had packed a smallish bag and left. He had been out buying himself a new suit and she had simply taken a boat south and stayed with friends. Oh, he had pestered her all right when he discovered her once after a concert; but she left for England, which was safer still since he didn't have the fare, and though he wrote long pleading letters and short terse ones he had finally given up. "There," she murmurs in a motherly fashion, burrowing under the sheet. "There, there."

At breakfast she is gay. Some weight has been lifted or curiosity sated. She talks rapidly and richly with Miss Charlton (relaxing morals) and Marge Ellis (rising food prices) and is conscious of a huge benignity as she hurls smiles and words, some of which are caught by Mr Armitage and Mr Romney at the next table. It's all cosy. All hunkydory. They chat across space informally in this over-big white dining-room.

Mr Dorahy is late coming down.

Constraint devils them when he appears, for by now all know what happened at the hall. But despite his blackened eye, his good-morning and his gentle smile are the same as ever as he unfolds his napkin and peers at the menu.

"Spot of bother last night?" asks crass Armitage. He is a pot-belly and large with nonsense.

"Only a spot." Dorahy smiles again directly into the other man's eyes.

"What were you on about, mate?"

Dorahy hesitates. He doesn't know whether to answer or not. Finally he says, "Something that happened here twenty years ago. You must remember."

"Bit long ago to rake up, isn't it?"

"No." He orders poached eggs.

Romney says, "It's too bloody long ago." He marmalades his toast savagely. And the savagery is detected.

Dorahy accuses, "Then you know to what I'm referring."

"If you mean that bloody nonsense down at Mandarana, then yes, I do."

"You call it nonsense! Seven people were killed."

"Blacks!" says Romney shortly. He takes a bite of his toast.

"There were other things. Lunt . . ." He stops himself. "Jesu Christe," he thinks. "Why go on?" He reaches for the butter and spreads himself a piece of toast too.

"Don't talk to me about Lunt," Romney blurts. He takes a swig of tea and it dribbles. "No one but a fool would have held on to that property of his as long as he did. Got out far too late. A mug, he was. Plain mug."

Dorahy is sick with the spasm of fury that takes him. He puts down his knife and grips hard at the seat of his chair. His fingers are digging wood. He swallows the leapt-up words one by one as he tries to gauge the truth of the two faces opposite him. This gristle is too much. He chokes and coughs and the eggs arrive.

The fabric of what passes for his discretion he has ripped apart himself in this cool white room ungeared to fractious debate. He sees other rooms, teaching rooms where he has always exercised a mastery of self, meeting rooms with the Separation League in angry spate and himself cool. Now, cutting brutally into his eggs and watching the yolk spurt out, he is conscious of his sixty-odd years and failure at the end after all. Projects unfinished, projects contemplated but not even begun, rise like iron men to deride. But he would complete this, he now decides. He would have the town recognise its martyr, relegating himself to a serving position without pain, for he has never been of the stuff from which saints are made.

"If there is one thing," he says, his innards constipatedly tight with tension, "that Lunt was not is mug. Not mug. He was unlucky from the start, but he never took his spleen out on others. He was generous, do you understand? Generous and forgiving. He could have given his life."

Armitage shoves his chair back impatiently. "You talk a lot of shit!" he retorts contemptuously. His belly swells with rage as well. Coming all this way to be preached at by some bloody unfrocked nun! A nancy. A bloodless man.

"Girlie," he calls to the waitress, "more toast, please."

"HANDS UP," Dorahy had said, "the boys who have not prepared this prose."

Eight hands were raised.

"All of you!" he marvelled. "Not one! Well," he said sadly, his snaggle teeth exposed in a disillusioned smile, "you will have to be punished. Line up!"

He rooted in the corner press and took out a cane which he wiped down with his right hand, lingeringly assessing the shape and the pliancy of it. It was all parody. All burlesque. The boys wore half-grins as comic Dorahy passed down the line of them giving the lightest of sarcastic taps to each outstretched palm.

When he reached young Buckmaster he did not even bother with the tap. Ironically, dismissively, he brushed him to one side with the most offensive of negligent plays of the stick. The boy turned scarlet as the master moved on flicking parodically at the next two outflung hands, and his hate, which had been till then a nebulous affair, crystallised into the stubborn matter that he would bear vengefully through to his middle age.

Dorahy was unaware. Perhaps. Their enmity, though tacit, had long been sensed mutually.

The boys returned to their places and Dorahy, wearily, despairingly, took up his chalk and began scribbling the work upon the board. The grains of it, the choking whiteness of it, saturated his whole being, and the phlegm he coughed anguishedly at the beginning of each day was a purging more of the spirit than the lungs. His hands dusty with it, he wiped drily along the seams of his trousers, slapped till small clouds arose. Looking through the classroom window for a moment while the boys painfully took down his fair copy, he could feel that the whole landscape, right down to the seaward fence, was chalk. He sighed.

He remembers this now, standing uncertainly outside the building where once . . . He debates entry, overcome by the newness of the teaching block, the horrible assurance of small garden plots and shrubs. The room where he had taught is still standing, a warped agglomeration of white-anted timber by the far fence, and he aches and does not ache to enter it once more and taste the flavour of lost baking summer days. Chanting comes from the rooms nearest him. The deadly Gregorian of rote. He pushes half-heartedly at the school gate, wondering how he will introduce himself, and walks slowly, sobered, along the gravel path towards the first of the buildings.

The headmaster is young. He is a mathematician. He lacks humour and poetry. When Dorahy has introduced himself, has explained himself, his stiffness wavers above the mess of time-tables and lesson-notes that form the lyric of his days. He offers a few minutes from his grudging muse and goes out with Dorahy into the hot sun.

"We use it as a store-room now," he says looking at the tottering building towards which they are heading. "Old book stock, new supplies, craft material for the boys. But it's had its day, I'm afraid. The school council recommends that it be pulled down next summer to make way for a new primary room."

Dorahy wipes sweat from his forehead and gapes at his past. The headmaster unlocks the padlock and draws back the bolt and, as he pushes open the splintered door, a staleness of air and memory takes Dorahy by the throat. He walks past the dull young rules man at his side and stands, more or less, as packing-cases allow, in the approximate geography of the dream, gazing out the cobwebby window to the smartness of acalypha beds along the fence-line.

"It was here," he says, "just here. I taught them Livy. A little Wordsworth. It seems so long ago. None of them particularly apt, you know, but I hoped it might have given them something."

"Hardly practical," the brash young headmaster says with a laugh, "for boys in a place like this."

"The sentimental old fool," he is thinking. "Taking up my morning." He fidgets impatiently.

Dorahy does not hear him. He is disturbed to the point of tears

101

by it all, by the deadly melancholy of fusty textbook piles, the worn bladders of footballs, the stacks of broken unusable desks.

"Just here," he repeats, recalling young Jenner's scrubbed morning face and the middle-aged sobriety of him now. And he says, smiling directly into the headmaster's eyes, *"Eheu fugaces, Postume, Postume, Labuntur anni . . ."*

"Of course, of course," the younger man mouths, not understanding. And "Well?" he says questioningly, giving a half-turn towards the door.

"Could you leave me here? Just a few minutes?" Dorahy asks. "I'd like to spend a little time. On my own," he adds.

The headmaster is appalled. He fears sentiment and mentally pig-roots like a nervous horse.

"I'm afraid not," he replies. He dangles his key meaningfully, giving the hint, and smiles. There is a boy he has to punish, he remembers.

Opening the door wide so that it cannot be ignored, he waits for the older man who is still trapped in the pity of the past. Those firm, eager or reluctant faces, he recalls, the marrow of my mornings.

Young Jenner grins at him fleetingly and says, "It's true, sir. You did add up," while Freddie Buckmaster scowls sulkily by the window. "Thank you, young Jenner," he says, and the mathematician, hearing his mumbles, squirms with shame for the old dodderer.

"There's nothing more you'd like to see?" he asks hopefully as they walk back once more to the main building.

"No. No. Thank you," Dorahy says.

The building has disowned him, he knows, the very ground that knew his feet. The whole of the morning is a plague of sunlight that threatens to beat him senseless.

"It's a mistake to come back," he admits and points ambiguously to his blackened eye about which the unimaginative other had not even wondered.

Their hands meet in the most counterfeit of gestures and Dorahy, turning his back on it all, goes, almost at a stumble, into the decorous, unfeeling street.

On that fourth day Snoggers Boyd calls round at the Sea Rip Hotel.

He finds Dorahy once again mooning along the water-front, a book in his hand. Some kind of tic obsesses his right eye as if it were a coefficient of anger. The blue of sky and water is violently peaceful and the island floating above the horizon looks like a close nirvana—except for the sun, which is a blistering outrage of heat.

They walk along the sandy front together to a seat under a couple of bunched palms.

"I have another favour to ask." Dorahy looks humble and his blackened eye makes his face a comic mask.

"Ah, yes," Boyd says, dreading. "What is it?"

"I've been doing some hard thinking. No. I haven't given up. Quite the reverse, in fact. I'd like you to publish an article for me."

Boyd takes quite a time filling his pipe. "What about?" he asks, then, "No. Don't tell me. I can guess."

Dorahy smiles. "The bile is low this morning. But only quiescent because of this—this idea. You could do it, you know. You're running that series called 'After Twenty Years' with all those low-keyed profiles of prominent figures. Fair enough, isn't it, to include one on Lunt? It could be the most exciting of the lot. 'Why I Left Town, by a victim.'" Dorahy finds bitterness has an actual taste.

"That's up to Lunt, surely."

"Not really. It's part of local history. You know it is."

Boyd draws hard on his pipe. He is no lover of the town's powers and, as a cool man, has always taken an onlooker's part. He has only to report, and he has always been canny enough to report without bias. He knows well which side his bread is buttered. Yet something about the suggestion—after all he is Dorahy's age—stirs unused wings. He sees headlines—A LITTLE INCIDENT AT THE LEAP, TOWN BORN IN VIOLENCE. All the trashy artifices of his employment could, with an almost amusing virulence, tear down the pretensions of Buckmaster and Sweetman. The interesting thing about it, he reflects, is that the whole town knew at the time but was never prepared to make outright challenges. It let things seep below the surface until they were finally covered with all the glosses of time.

To bring them up again now would—what?

Despite himself he starts to chuckle. "We could run pictures as well," he says. "Freddie Buckmaster with caption 'Vigilante Settles Down' or Barney Sweetman as the avenging power!"

Dorahy says quietly, "Why don't you?"

"Oh, my God, my dear Tom. It's impossible. The laws of libel for one thing. The election for another. You don't seem to realise the voters don't want to be jolted. They're happy with things as they are. Change is a threat, a worry. They'd resent me for it."

"Does that matter?"

"The laws of libel matter."

"You could get around that. Do it without names—except for Lunt's. After all, you were there with me. We came in on the end of things."

Boyd remembers the heat, the body, the high rock but can only protest, "In God's name what good will all this serve?"

"It will ease my itch."

"*Your* itch? What a bloody fake philanthropist are you! I suspect you don't really give tuppence for Lunt. It's a personal vendetta on Buckmaster and his mob."

Dorahy looks away from the other man across the water. He knows him to be right and admits, "You're partly correct, you know. I confess. *Mea culpa.* But I do give more than tuppence for Charlie. Truly. His name has been shut out of the town as though he were a public sinner. Is that fair? Is it fair to force a man to make himself a hermit just to save the faces of others? Because that is what has happened."

"I know. I know all this. And it might be interesting to rock the boat at that." He keeps toying with the idea.

"You've never rocked the boat."

"True. But if I were to—I say if—I wouldn't be doing it for you. I don't much like being—having been—a yes-man all these years. You grind my nose in it."

"Save your soul," Dorahy urges eagerly. "Go against the grain."

Boyd is pensive. He knocks out his pipe on the heel of his shoe.

"I'm on the point of retirement," he says, "after a blameless thirty years. There's nothing more they can do to me. We've thought of going south in another year or so." He is arguing aloud with himself with Dorahy straining for his predicate.

"Then you'll do it," he demands rather prematurely. The world is a giddy blue.

"I'll think about it," Boyd says. "That's all I promise you, but I promise you that."

L OST BETWEEN voyages in his own port, Snoggers sits, green eye-shaded, pencil at the ready, his inner man torn between doing and not-doing, between the validity of what Dorahy had demanded and the folly of it, the senselessness perhaps.

He'd kept a column and a half blank for the last of his series and wanted, insipidly, to do the right thing by everybody. Lucy with her calm and candour had urged him. "Do it," she had said. "Make it your final testament." Which is what it would be, he muses, with Buckmaster's re-election coming up.

Perhaps Lucy is still in love with Lunt. He wonders about this, staring idly at the calendar facing him on the far wall, and writes a line or two, transposes its high-pitched whinge down a third and re-reads. Balderdash! Slop! A minor irritant only unless he takes the bull by its ionic horns and slams home with all his power. Significance. That is the word. How tie in so that the significance of what he is doing with what he has already done has a total qualitative force like a battering ram's?

Ram all right, he recalls, grinning, thinking of Sweetman's amorous but tangential approaches to Lucy one long-forgotten Christmas when Sweetman had drunkenly seemed all hands and phallus. She had laughed at him with such genuine amusement it still hurt to envision Sweetman's crumpled foolish mask, the watery pathos of his myopic eyes.

Munching his morning-tea biscuit Boyd tries again. His thick tongue pursues crumbs in teeth inlets and something begins to ache sharply and persistently—soul? tooth? Glancing out the office window, he takes solace from the hachured sky beyond the palm. The evident blue seems infinite, is so; and as he writes again the words wrenched out of amusement and pain come more easily. Comfortably he has the sense of the world itself being unreal, and that makes what he is doing easier. And without venom, he jubilates, decoding fluidly and reasonably from memories he had thought long lost. Reasonably, he reassures himself. It must move reasonably. And he has another biscuit that he bites absent-mindedly without realising he is eating at all.

His mind keeps browsing among other pastures of the last two decades. That first ten years when he brought out the weekly broadsheet single-handed; the second when it became a daily and he had one man assist him with the press while he did all the reporting, writing, editing on his own. He has a backstop now and a cadet, but he is even more tired and is looking forward to the limbo of retirement.

Shaking himself into the present, he is, getting up restless from his chair, scratching around and coming back to re-read what he has written. Words come readily to Boyd—and that is his problem—to prevent that free flow from becoming merely the banal or the trite. He scores out a phrase or two and reads again, a little smile curling his mouth. It is difficult not to make Lunt look like the sacrificial lamb.

Mid-morning knocks on his sunny door bringing the head of Dorahy peering round. It is the fifth day and he is avoiding like the plague the hideous brouhaha of a grand picnic luncheon at the show-ground. Everyone seems to have gone while he is sticking it solitarily out for the week, enduring Romney and Armitage with their breakfast and dinner-time grunts. He is still a misfit and wears his blackened eye like a badge, while the town reinforces his Ishmael qualities after twenty years, stresses his unpalatability.

"Well then," he says to Boyd, "a good morning to you. Am I disturbing anything?"

"Nothing much." Boyd has decided not to tell Dorahy yet of his article. He slips the papers under a blotter. "Just routine stuff. Have a seat."

Dorahy pulls out the chair facing him. There are no *arrière-pensées* on the squarish face confronting him, no deviousness in the eye.

"It must be all in the heart," he says, concluding his thoughts aloud.

"What is?" Boyd is transparently curious.

"Nothing." Dorahy hesitates. "Have you given any more thought to what I asked?"

"I have," Boyd says.

"And are you going ahead?"

"I haven't decided."

"But there isn't much time, man!" Dorahy's heart suddenly plunges into a panic beating. "Half the week's over."

"Yes."

"Well?"

"I've given it thought, Tom. Quite a lot of thought. But let me do things my own way, will you?"

"It's always ultimately been the thinkers or the writers who get things done," Dorahy says petulantly. "Men of violence hardly ever score."

"True."

"And again well?"

"Look," Boyd cries impatiently, resenting his conversion, "leave it will you? I'm still thinking about it. And by the way, Lucy has asked you for dinner tonight. Just a few people, the Jenners, Gracie. Lunt is staying over till the end of the week."

"It will be pleasant," Dorahy says, "not to watch Romney slopping his mess of pottage. Thank you. And don't come for me. I'll walk over."

Outside the office of the *Gazette,* the streets are flush with visitors who can be recognised by their curiosity and a happiness that comes from living there no longer, Dorahy ponders cynically as he steps along the pavement with them. Here and there—the face on the coin—he recognises and waves or occasionally pauses to go through the same questions and greetings, explain away his eye and say in chorus How long for? Since when? Oh, marvellous, marvellous to see you, Hasn't changed much has she, the old town? and he cannot bear this Calvary.

He returns to the tea-room he first visited, hoping to find the girl there who at last smiled. She's still washing down the bar counter, but she knows him now and says, "Well, how's it going?"

Dorahy gives her his gappy smile and says, "I'm afraid not too well."

She is sympathetic. "That's the trouble, isn't it?" she says. "Things are never so good when you see them again."

There is a raw wisdom about her.

"You're so right," he says. "Nothing has changed really. I mean the people who were still here when I left so long ago. I had hoped for—

well, something. A gentleness perhaps. Or richer thinking. Or penitence."

He is almost talking to himself and the girl says, "It's tea you like, isn't it? I'll get you some."

This time there are no apparitions of the spirit. Young Jenner does not emerge to counsel. Perhaps, reasons Dorahy, the present reality submerges memory. He sees young Jenner now as the man he has become, much of the eagerness rubbed off him so that he appears in the garb of all his thirty-six years merely as sober and sensible. Dorahy sighs for it, and his sigh is interrupted by the arrival of tea.

Facing the door from one of the rickety tables, he sips and watches the street. The smallish palms down the centre of the road throw blue shadows and it is across one of these patches that he sees the older Buckmaster stride, ripping apart morning. Dorahy wishes himself invisible but the other has spotted him and comes to the doorway of the café.

Yes. He knows them all. Booms to the girl and pockets her good-morning as his right. Exploding what little peace there was about Dorahy, he draws up an uninvited chair.

"I thought you might have gone by now," he offers tactlessly. "Seen all you wanted to."

"You're using the wrong verb," sour Dorahy says. "Done, not seen."

He regrets his spleen. It only serves to alert.

Buckmaster is chewing this over.

"Why don't you go back?" he asks, genuinely curious. "That or fall in with the spirit of it, eh? Why I've just left the happiest crowd I've seen in years out at the show-ground. Massive picnic. Ring events. Side shows. The lot. They love it and they're loving each other." He presents himself reasonably, his large wine-stained face seeking sense for the moment.

"You know why."

"But that's over, a long time ago. God, you make it all repetitious. Can't you see that? Not even Lunt wants it. You're trying to make him something he rejects, a figure of pity twenty years too late. No man wants that."

"I don't see him as a figure of pity. Nor myself. But I do see you and Sweetman as figures of violence."

Buckmaster's complexion deepens. "Girlie," he calls, "bring us some more tea, will you?

"Look," he says, turning a curiously worn countenance on Dorahy, "let's talk this out, man to man. There are things I regret. Naturally. Every man has those. But I—all of us—have been trying to live those moments down. No one's proud of them. They just happened in a natural course of events. It's part of history."

"History has two faces."

"What do you mean?"

"I mean your view may not necessarily be the right view. There's another side to it. I want the other side to be seen."

"After all this time you still believe that?"

"Yes."

Buckmaster gulps at his tea. "Then there's nothing I can say that will bring you to your senses."

"I'm very much in them."

Buckmaster says gently, "You're not, you know."

This seems to bring a temporary peace between them. Both of them smoke in silence; but it is a false peace and Dorahy is the one who cracks.

He says, "There's not much time left, is there? For living, I mean."

Buckmaster looks up at his fanatic face and there is a total weariness on his own.

"That's what I've been trying to say," he says.

YOUR FULL name is Thomas Wade Dorahy? the magistrate asked.

Yes.

And you are teacher in charge of the provisional school at The Taws?

Yes.

And how long have you held this position?

Three years.

Have you been, the magistrate asked, his face keen with the prospect of a new witness, a member of the so-called Separation League?

I have.

And for how long?

Two years.

Would you consider two years, Mr Sheridan pursued, a long enough period in which to know the other members of the league?

I thought we were here to discuss—

In good time, Mr Dorahy, the magistrate said. I am asking you questions that may have pertinence. Please answer the question.

Yes, I would, Mr Dorahy said. He was inclined to truculence.

And did you consider that your membership of this group required certain loyalties from you?

Mr Dorahy hesitated. It would depend on the nature of the matter.

The nature?

Yes. Whether the pursuits on which the league was engaged were likely to conflict with conscience.

I see. Mr Sheridan took a long look at the dour string of a fellow.

110

And was there ever such an occasion—where there was a conflict of conscience?

Yes.

I take it you are referring to incidents on the twenty-fourth of June at Mount Mandarana?

I am.

Were you in fact a member of the reprisal team?

No.

Then you admit you would not have complete knowledge of the actual events of that day?

Mr Dorahy squeezed his hands tightly together. I saw enough.

That is not quite the same thing, you agree?

Mr Dorahy was silent.

Well, Mr Sheridan asked more loudly, do you agree?

I suppose so.

What actual events did you witness on that day, Mr Dorahy? Tell us in your own words.

Mr Dorahy cleared his throat. He could feel a trembling beginning.

On that morning on which I suspected there might be some active reprisal against the Lindeman tribe, we rode north to Mandarana to see if we could prevent what we imagined might happen.

We?

Mr Jenner, his son and myself.

Go on.

We came round by the western base of the mountain in time to see Mr Boyd who had been a member of the party bending over a dead lubra.

And who was this?

A young woman called Kowaha.

You knew her? Mr Sheridan asked with horrible interest.

Yes. I had given her food on a number of occasions.

And for what reason?

None—except that she asked. Mr Dorahy went red with indignation at the implication.

And how had this lubra come to die, do you think?

She appeared to have fallen from the cliff. She had her baby with her.

And was the baby alive?

111

It was.

Would you imagine, Mr Dorahy, Mr Sheridan asked playing a small five-finger exercise on the edge of his desk, that the gin might have been helped to her death? Pushed say?

I don't know.

But you must have some idea. You say you know these men well enough after two years to assess a situation.

You are leading me, Dorahy protested. She was morally pushed, that's all I can say.

Ah! Then you admit you have no grounds for accusation of any violence at all against the members of the Separation League?

No. That's not true.

In that case how many dead did you see?

Only one.

The woman?

Yes.

Then you had no knowledge of what had actually occurred on the peak of Mandarana?

No. Yes. What I heard. Mr Dorahy was beginning to babble. You forget I found Lunt. Found him a week after these events. There was that as well. Violence like that. Oh, my God!

You must control yourself, Mr Dorahy, the magistrate said. He took a slow and careful sip from a glass of water. Mr Lunt has declined to give evidence. Suspicions, opinions are not facts and must not be brought forward in this court.

This is rubbish, nonsense! Dorahy cried out. You cannot allow justice to miscarry like this.

Mr Dorahy, the magistrate intervened, his face bright with anger, the court must not be addressed in this way. Unless you can control yourself I must ask you to stand down.

Control myself! Dorahy cried. Oh, my God! Control! His face began to stream with tears.

Through the glaze of them he observed young Buckmaster smiling at his father.

Mr Sheridan was enormously embarrassed. I must ask the witness to stand down, he said.

BOYD HAS put his press to sleep. "It's done," he thinks and looks at a pull of his main story. Read in cold blood, it is far more drastic than he had imagined it would be. "Oh God," he thinks, "but it's done now! The wolves will be onto my sled while Lucy and I brave it out." Sweetman smilingly benign before election time will have his face changed for him. But how will the public react, he wonders. Put their money on the old favourite? Sweetman is out there wearing Buckmaster's colours and riding hard to win.

He rubs his palms together a little at this, feels the sweat skate between them, mops his neck and face with his handkerchief and gives a tuneless little whistle. His backstop, Madden, is putting the next day's issue together in the back room. Nothing can go back now. Only forward. Trumpets blaring, the troops on the move and Lunt, Dorahy and himself facing the blast of them alone on a high hill. Or valley, is it? Gully? Not even the dignity of height.

"I've wanted," he thinks, "to do something like this for years."

He slips the pull into an envelope and shoves it in his coat pocket. He roars, "Madden!" and the young rabbit face of his assistant peers gap-mouth round the door.

"I'll be out for about an hour. When McKay comes back tell him to hold the fort, will you? I'll be back soon."

The street is blistering but it is only a short distance to the Sea Rip. Glare and sun work away at him and even panama'd he feels the bite of northern light. His eyes squint. The heat does not lick but rasp. Excited, nervous at what he has done, looking forward to seeing the

113

last of the town with his gesture so firmly behind him: he will be able to do nothing but leave.

He passes Buckmaster who is leaving some café on the main street and they wave cheerios that will never be waved again. Already he has a sense of homesickness and observes with the eyes of the newly arrived or the about to leave. There's sadness in the docks at the end of the street, the boats pulled in from journeys on blue water, masts somehow thin.

Dorahy is only fifty yards ahead of him.

He saunters, then, to let him get back to the hotel. No point in having the day pronounce them to the roaring world. He wanders down to the water-front where peelings and papers wash round the piles and, watching the thick syrup of water slap and pull at the wharf, he has a slow smoke.

Dorahy, his glasses making him older and more benign, is lying on his bed reading when Boyd finally gets there. There was a gay party on the front terrace of the pub with Gracie Tilburn queening it over a bevy of drones. Waves. Cries. The party envisioned now as he gazes down on the solitary Dorahy who has uttered nothing but a little grunt since he said, "Come in."

"I've got something here you might like to read," Boyd says, pulling the envelope from his coat pocket, and tossing it, an unconsidered trifle, onto the counterpane.

Dorahy slings his long skinny legs over the side of the bed and sits up. "You've done it?" he hopes aloud. Unfolding and then reading, his face changing with each line. The shock of it! Even the forgivable journalese! He reads the last few lines aloud and gives a great cry:

"At last! And no one named. It's a miracle of circumlocution. No. Hardly that. Of discretion. Oh, my God, Snoggers, it's more than I wanted! More!"

There are tears somewhere. Each man looks away from the weakness in Dorahy, struck to the pith of him, and Dorahy gets up and goes to stand at the veranda door of his room. He is gazing across the water to the island. The dozens of blues. The island sky-floating above its own shadow. Isolated laughter from the terrace below. It is as if he is prepared to drown now in blue, the end being here at last.

"You've done it for me," he says turning to look at Boyd, with the weakness safely out of sight.

"No. Not for you, Tom. It's my own gesture. Sorry to take the

114

credit from you. But truly I have done it for me. Some rash beneath the skin. It is dying now, with this."

"What do you think will happen?" Dorahy is eager as a child.

"Who knows? There's a final get-together in the hall tomorrow. Last night and all that. You and Lunt would be crazy to go. Buckmaster will have all the speeches organised. Stay out of it. You've made your point already."

"You've made it," Dorahy says. "I was only reporting. It will finish you, I suppose," he adds reflectively.

But Snoggers will be carrying a swag of victims with him.

"Do you mind? Really mind?"

"At the moment I'm too exalted with the excitement of it. Later, well, I don't know about that. Can't say. Already I feel the griefs of farewell."

Dorahy is silent, then he says, "I feel guilty about that. Truly. But settled with God, somehow."

"Or the devil," Boyd suggests. "You are a real *agent provocateur*."

"Maybe. Who knows? Who really knows? . . . Would you like a drink? Have you time or isn't it wise?"

"It's unwise, but I'll have one."

The darkness of the bar-room, its docile shadows, peels some of the age from their faces. They talk of nothings—the heat, the landscape, the last few days—and are halfway through their drinks when Sweetman and young Buckmaster walk in. They are the eclipse of the soul.


The noon door of Boyd's office has, with its closed-for-lunch sign, a vulnerable innocence that persists even after he has let himself in. The street outside is practically empty except for a dog lifting its leg against one of the *Gazette* hoardings. A passing comment, thinks Boyd. Just wait till tomorrow. Madden is still folding in the back room and is halfway through the issue, perspiring languidly with his shifty rabbit face bent in a whitened concentration over his work.

Boyd takes the completed papers and piles them on a trestle slide against the back window, thinks better of it and locks them in a press.

"When you've finished," he advises the crouching Madden, "lock the rest in as well, will you?"

He goes back to the front room and looks out the door at the dusty, decent street with its knobs of palms. Nothing moves. Is he imagining the lull? Then around the corner a dray rumbles and creaks past as he stands there watching and blinking. Just outside the horse drops its sweet-smelling dung. If he were a man searching for omens then he could find this lucky and could even grin. Chickens' innards, the movement of wild stars, the way counters fall. But he recalls unexpectedly the whiteness of Madden's down-bent face prosily withdrawn as he folds and stacks, folds and stacks, and on some uncrystallised impulse goes down the passage to the back room and stands regarding him for a few speculative moments. He does not look up. Why? Boyd wonders, with an unreasonable spurt of irritation.

"Here," he says, testily, "I'll give you a hand. We should get them finished by three." He curses McKay for being still out at the town picnic reporting the follies.

They work in the heat and the silence into which the clock drops its seconds like blows. The tap over the basin drips unrhythmically. Irritable, after fifteen minutes, with a kind of abrading curiosity, Boyd stops his automaton hands and regards his backstop, notes the indifferent pallor, the sparse stringy hair, the unhealthy flush of some skin disorder erupting on the starved-looking angles of the jaw.

"Have you had a look through it?" he asks.

Madden's spidery hands hesitate in their work, but he refuses to look up. He knows the reason behind the question and has not yet discovered his own true reaction in the matter. Stalling, he says carefully, "Had a glance." The hands have not once disrupted the rhymes of work—fold, press, fold, press, stack.

Boyd is cautious, too. This will test his loyalty, he decides, about which he has long had his doubts. The boy on the burning deck, Horatio at the bridge. All the troubadours of fealty singing together.

"Tell me, Joe," he persists, "what did you think of my centre-page story? The one on Mandarana?"

At this moment, Madden is not anybody's man, though he is a white-corpuscled fellow with the seeds of treachery bred into him. His pay is low enough for him to be suborned by anyone at all. Wageless and gutless. There have been past occasions when money has produced bogus red cells of a meretricious attachment. He grins uneasily, remembering.

"Fair enough."

"Dangerous?"

"I wouldn't know."

116

Boyd places another folded paper very delicately on the pile: he is a man in whom the most vast of angers produces only the most antithetic response.

"But you must have some idea," he argues softly. "Do you think I am pushing it too far?"

"Maybe."

"Then you know the background of all this? The things I've left unstated?"

Madden's pimples appear to flare. He says, "I've heard a thing or two."

"So."

The hands resume their work while clock and tap wrestle it out and in the superficial air of truce Boyd gradually decides that he doesn't trust Madden although they have worked five years together. "Printer's devil!" he decides.

He is right not to trust. At some unspecified hour of concealing dusk Madden, with a discarded copy of the next day's *Gazette* folded small inside his shirt, seeks out Buckmaster to satisfy unformulated notions of preferment that he bears like an inner rash. If he wanted outrage, then he has it, observing the passionate explosions on the face of the reading man. Foolishly, Buckmaster cannot control his rantings and Madden grows small with fear and satisfaction.

"I won't forget . . . will make amends . . . take my word . . . a promise a promise . . . very shortly you will be . . ." he raves to his shrinking stooge. While despising.

Madden can only smile and tremble with the excitement of disloyalty that has never bought him anything really yet. As he returns to dusk, his devious compulsions satisfied, he is perplexed by the inner emptiness that overtakes him.

BETWEEN THE steak and the orange mousse, the flirta-
tious warblings of Gracie Tilburn and the more sombre
conversation of the Jenners, Boyd becomes so conscious of an op-
pressive, almost sonorous quality of evil that he feels he cannot com-
municate, even on the flattest levels, with his guests. He pushes his
chair back under his wife's anxious eye and says, "You'll have to excuse
me for a little. I have this persistent feeling that things are not all
right at the office. Don't ask me to explain right now, but I'll have to
go back there to check up." His fat-creased eyes are unhappy.

"Take me with you," Dorahy suggests. There is a moment's silence.
Lunt questions with raised eyebrows, and finally, "No," says Boyd.
"No. Not for this."

He leaves them while the pudding wilts. Outside, beyond the curiosity of their eyes, his own tension runs wild for a few seconds. Only
a mile from town, he decides quickly that saddling the horse will not
be worth it and sets off at a fat man's jog-trot, his heart knocking and
his lungs soon announcing the pain. Gasping, he slows down to a
walk and as he comes to the last straight stretch before the stores
begin, he sees that which he has dreaded.

Fire is all rose and gold, excitement and orange joy, leaping and
threatening, with blacker centres to flames than the heart could imagine. Its appetite increases with the reds and yellows, a hunger to paint
colour all over a street's canvas. Its sound is animal and high-pitched
and Boyd, who has seen its menacing light long before he hears its
voice, knows exactly where it is and why. There are ghoul watchers
already by the time he arrives and he can see, even from across the

118

road, that someone has bashed in the front door to his office and that the room at the back is fully ablaze. He races ahead of his throbbing shadow across to the pulse of it, but the heat is too strong and strikes him back again and again. The smell of spirits is still in the air.

He retreats to the knot of watchers and someone—friend?—says, "They've sent for the fire boys, Snoggers. The hoses should be here in a minute."

Helpless he is, standing watching the work of a life-time gobbled in moments. They are all agape with it, and by now there are children in night-wear yelping with festival. Flames throw wild light on the faces of the crowd, and Boyd, illuminated like a saint, prays, "Christ, oh, Christ, let them hurry!"

Time crawls in deliberate collusion with the speed of the flames now mounting in spiralling peaks above the shop's eaves. Boyd, who is insane with suspicion, wonders have the firemen been suborned, when suddenly the dray lurches round a bend of the street. When the water starts to pour the crowd gives out its bestial sigh. Of regret? Boyd wonders viciously, for the shop next to his had been starting to catch and the crowd was being denied its bread and circuses with every conquering hiss of water-play. The two hoses are turned against the scarlet heart of it all which burns and slows, burns and slows. It is controlled within minutes, but the hoses have come too late, Boyd knows. Slushing through puddles to his burnt-out front office, he is conscious only of black ash and water, the rubble of twenty-five years accumulating behind his rage and hopelessness. He would weep but for the watchers, and defiantly pushes his coughing way through smoke denser in the outer room, where he can still make out the ruined press and near it the clotted, reeking pile of the next day's issue.

He gives the smouldering heap a kick and sparks and smoke fly out.

"That's all it would have been, anyway," he thinks sourly. "Sparks and smoke." A miserable fireworks at that, a fizzer, followed by a lot of political obscurantism.

He walks more slowly through the wreckage back to the front of the office and it is not amusing, not even faintly and hysterically funny, when a renewed blast from the hose hits him with such a wallop he is knocked to the ground.

Through this sour comedy he hears Buckmaster's voice giving directions. "Hold it, you fellows," he is saying kindly. "You've hit Boyd. There now, spin it over this way."

Boyd scrambles to his feet, his clothing a mush, and he walks to the sound of the voice on the edge of the crowd and his eyes catch Buckmaster's and hold them.

"Administering the sacraments, too," he says.


"We should have insisted on going with him," Dorahy says, addressing himself to the Jenners and Lunt.

Dinner is over and he is standing in the long living-room facing the others who are seated near the window. They are all conscious of the revival of a long-lost warmth that both soothes and disturbs. Gracie has ceased examining young Jenner's wife for flaws, and loves both of them, while Lucy for the second time in their lives takes Lunt's hand and extends the other to Dorahy, embracing him as well. Her anxiety reaches out for the significance of hand-clasps, the touch of eyes.

Lunt says tiredly, "Will someone tell me exactly what is going on? I feel you others know."

Lucy releases his hand and swings in her chair to face him, to disturb his resignation.

"Only Tom knows," she says. "It's the paper. Tomorrow's. There's an article about you and the trouble at Mandarana."

Lunt laughs harshly. "So long ago!" he cries. "He didn't ask me. Didn't ask whether I'd mind."

"Should he have?" someone asks.

"I think so," Lunt says. "I do think so. I haven't come back here to make trouble. Tom talked me into coming back, God knows how. I don't want the mess it's turned out to be."

Dorahy says pacifically, "It's no good going over all that. It's done now and there's nothing we can do about it. It's my fault. Was my suggestion. Blame me if you like."

"You've made a lot of trouble," Lunt agrees. "Who's it going to help?"

For the first time in a week Dorahy is stringently honest.

"It's going to destroy," he admits. "Buckmaster. Sweetman. They'll be exposed for what they are."

"Do you think anyone really cares at this stage?" asks the older Jenner. "Do you?" He is as persistent as Dorahy.

"I hope so," Dorahy replies. "Oh, I hope so."

"An avenging angel," Lunt remarks. "You're mad, Tom. I mean that. Crazed for a wrong cause." He frowns. "And now Boyd thinks they've got wind of it, eh? Can't any of you realise that I've come back through love, not hate! Love!"

Dorahy's explanation is pithy. Lamp-light makes anything possible with its antiphon and response of flicker and flow. The clear glass mantles give definite truths—which subdue. They sit in silence after his words, listening to the night outside where there is nothing but the noises of insects in the viscous air and the looming authority of trees whose branches reach out and touch the three wide verandas of the house.

Restless, Dorahy walks out to the head of the garden steps that plunge into night-dark with the assurance of a swimmer. Like everything about this house, the steps are firm and resolute. The township is a mile away on the northern road and, examining the sky for portents, Dorahy could swear to orange light. He ponders fire, dismisses and reponders. The glow swells and fades. He goes down into the steady dark of the trees and walks though the scent of cane and frangipani to the road that runs with few curves back to the hub of it all. He can see nothing.

Yet returning to the veranda and looking back into the lighted room he does see something after all.

Gracie Tilburn is seated at the piano and is playing and singing "Auld Lang Syne." Her voice floats like a miracle on the waiting air. Young Jenner is absorbed in her. He might be sixteen again. And in the corner of the window bay Lucy and Lunt are sitting with hands clasped. They look at each other and no words come.

GRACIE TILBURN is soggy with tears.

Lonely in her hotel room, unassuaged by the banalities of small talk that have sustained her throughout the week, she gives way to an urge to weep that has been pressing at the back of her heart all day. Once yielded to, its luxury becomes addictive and she weeps for having wept, groping through oceans of regret, a baffled swimmer who has lost track of the life-line. There has been a concert (successful), several women's afternoon teas (tepid), and three private dinners at homes where the male guests were reluctant to flirt under their wives' noses.

She is weeping for Tim Jenner and the loss of him—that is, the loss of the sensitivity of him. She won't credit him with having aged and sees him devoured by family cares—though at the concert she could have sworn that he was regarding her as he had once regarded her while she sang. Blinkered, he is. Like some dray horse that looks neither right nor left, strains on the load, and pulls and pulls and goes forward between worlds of happening without a sideways glance. The fool!

But is she any happier for having glanced sideways too often? She gulps noisily at this thought and hears an unexpected knock on her bedroom door with rage. How terrible she must be looking with the practical ravages of grief all over her person registering a kind of monochrome complaint!

She does quick things to her face and hair before the spotty mirror, straightens skirt and blouse, dabs powder wherever, and re-thinks herself as she opens the door on Boyd, who is standing in an attitude of submission. To what? she wonders.

He is surprised by her puff-ball face, usually so elegantly clad in clichés. Flesh is making its own admissions and he drops his eyes to conceal their first flash of curiosity before inspecting her frankly.

"Hullo," he says. "I'm lucky to find you."

"Home-sick." She explains her face away. "For here and there."

"Coming back's the devil, isn't it?" he comments, aware of her lie, and hesitates before he says, "Lucy and I won't be able to join you here for dinner this evening after all." It seems like a blow to her already punched-silly face. "I'm sorry," he says. "Lucy sends her love."

Gracie can feel the moulding of her face gradually return to its normal shape. She puts out both her hands. Words are never enough. Boyd catches them, though he had thought of giving them a miss—and begins to smile at the idea. Friendship is like trapeze artistry for gods of the high wire, he muses: one swings and the other, trusting in the first and in God, wheels over all sorts of abysses of mistrust to be caught firmly by welcoming hands. Or words. He would hate to let her drop, really. She is more vulnerable than ever with the lineal registrations of time upon her face.

"Never mind!" Gracie cries. "How kind of you to call! Would you care to have tea with me on the terrace before you go back?"

He doesn't care to, but he will. He says so. Her eyes widen with pleasure. She had not believed he would. Some piece of male, she thinks thankfully, any piece, in dutiful attendance. She gathers her bag and goes out with him into the hall which is full of gothic gloom, green light and polished cedar. The stair-case is almost baronial. Its curves meet their obliquity, there is a momentary clash and they descend side by side.

Gracie's face is fully remoulded. She will be able to be coy soon, and by the time they arrive at the antithesis of all this—wide green front, palms, blue water—she is recovered in full. In white, she thinks with non-sequitur vanity. I'm at my best in white. Women should wear lots of it. Hers, though crumpled from a passionate hurling of herself upon the bed, is frail and lovely. The creases are natural enough. She steers him to a table beyond the others who are having pre-luncheon drinks. Leaves grow over this end of the terrace, broad, green and sharp with light where Boyd seats her absent-mindedly and drags over a cane chair for himself. All the morning he has been supervising the clean-up of the wreckage in his office and is still numb. Dorahy and Lunt proceed endlessly past him, the fiasco of them both.

They amble through pleasantries for ten minutes, Gracie pouring his tea with what she believes to be old-world charm, and they gaze at each other less stiffly above the cups.

"Tell me, Gracie," he says, "do you remember the affair at Mandarana? I know you were only a girl then, but I thought perhaps you might."

She is astonished at the change in him during the very utterance. The roly-poly cheeks lose their bluntness. The eyes narrow.

"Of course. But it is twenty years ago now."

"That's what everyone says. Did you know Charlie Lunt at all in those days?"

"No. Not really. I knew who he was but that's all."

"Did you ever hear any talk about what happened to him?"

"Some. Some. But it's so long ago," she repeats. "It's hard to remember."

"What do you think really happened? I'm curious because my life's work here was destroyed last night as a kind of bitter result." He takes a sip of tea and it too is bitter on his tongue. He has no use for sugar.

"I only heard what you others heard. What Tim Jenner told me. How they cared for him. That sort of thing."

"Did he ever accuse anyone?" Boyd muses aloud.

Gracie shifts her chair into a bigger shade patch. "No," she says. "Never. Tim told me he wouldn't talk about it right from the very first."

Useless, Boyd thinks. Hopeless. Why do I care? Have I caught the itch from Dorahy? Certainly he is mad with anger over last night's disaster and now is beginning to assume the cloak of avenger as well. Is there no end to it?

Take this hotel. Any hotel. Place in it artificial scenes of welcome and farewell. Match the stain of easily wrung tears with the green wall-paint, and the laughter with glimpses of starched table linen, and still you have nothing. The impersonality is truly miraculous and you hate this for ever and all places like it. Against this backdrop Boyd prepares for a plunge.

He enlists Gracie's moral aid. Can he count on her? Does she believe in the essential evil of men like Buckmaster? She nods, only half-willingly, but she nods. Is that all? The nodding head? The acquiescent shoulders? On the last evening of all these false evenings will she plead for Lunt through actions however indirect?

124

Gracie is accustomed to deviousness of a more polished kind with only herself at stake. She is ignorant of how to act for others.

"How?" she asks. Boyd tells her. By refusing to sing. By giving reasons.

But the programme has been prepared, she counters. She can't do this. But she can, Boyd insists. Not only can. Must. For Lunt. For Dorahy. For himself.

It's male logic, she thinks. Totally self-involved.

"You know, I don't really like Tom Dorahy."

"You're not doing it for him alone. It's Lunt, Lunt."

"But I scarcely know Mr Lunt. And he doesn't want it done for him—twenty years too late."

"There's me," he says. "And the Jenners—Tim and his father believe in Lunt and the wrong done him. They were people you loved."

She is silent. The tea has grown cold and is still undrunk. Her relationship with Tim was once the slowly unfolded rose of her. Now it's the worm in the bud.

"If I could talk it over with him—Tim, that is." She hopes and Boyd understands more than he displays.

"I'll arrange it."

"It's too late now," she replies, meaning something else.

"It's never too late."

She comes suddenly to her senses. The gut of her is disturbed, but there is a coherence about this man speaking with her that makes her loves and fears seem paltry. She understands that he is seeking now more than vengeance for last night's blow, that he sees the town as seeded in disaster and brought forth as bitter fruit.

"Forgive me," she says with honesty this one time at least, coyness put away and the trumpery of it. "I'm thinking too much of me. I'll do whatever you wish."

Boyd leans across the table and takes her hand. The table rocks and tea slops in both saucers. It is comic at this moment. Boyd is fat, shapeless and unheroic to look at. His virtue is in his voice or his smile. He gives her both.

The treacle of summer. It filled the courtroom in glutinous waves. Mr Sheridan had gone so far as to remove his coat—and that without diffidence. He did some paper-shuffling, refilled his water glass from the jug.

So far as can be ascertained, he said, peering hard through his spectacles at the packed room, there is no certain evidence that Lieutenant Frederick Buckmaster acted altogether improperly in the affair at Mandarana on the twenty-fourth of June.

He paused to glare at Dorahy who had let out a snort of rage. No certain evidence, I said, and that I mean. My colleagues and I have sifted all the evidence brought before this select committee and our findings are that, while there were certain irregularities in the proceedings of that day, the entire unhappy events were the result of wrongly placed enthusiasm, a perhaps too nice sense of injustice and the understandable grievance of men who found the difficulties of living—and I mean pioneer living—aggravated to an unbearable pitch by the extra annoyance the blacks posed to their efforts.

Annoyances! hissed Dorahy. His hands were clasped so hard the knuckles ached, and the ache spread up his arms till it touched the acute perimeters of his mind. Unheeded, sweat dribbled its way down the nape of his neck. From outside the fragmented words of passers-by floated improperly in, to the annoyance of the magistrate who frowned and cleared his throat.

Hideously, Dorahy became aware that Lieutenant Buckmaster, seated down from him two rows and to the right, was beginning to grin. A twitch, like some frightful tic, attacked the schoolmaster's knee. He leant forward as Sheridan continued speaking.

While our findings tend to absolve Lieutenant Buckmaster from deliberate malice in the matter, nevertheless the court feels it must warn him against acting uncircumspectly or with undue haste in other matters of this kind. Distance, and consequent delay with the arrival of official advice, have had an adverse effect in the whole unfortunate business. However, Lieutenant Buckmaster is warned that in future he must not act without due consultation with his superiors, even if the delay seems impossibly difficult in the circumstances.

Warned! cried Dorahy over the shocked and packed room. Warned! He was on his feet babbling.

Mr Sheridan glanced at the assisting constable, who shoved his way along the rows until he could reach Dorahy.

A travesty! A farce! Dorahy kept shouting. Strong arms were propelling him to the aisle. Within the blur of faces round him only Buckmaster's shone with the greasy clarity of success. You! he cried incoherently. You you you!

As they got him outside into the brighter day, he could hear the magistrate resume his monotone summation.

You must try to keep calm, sir, the constable kept saying. He felt sorry for the silly coot. Try having a bit of a sitdown in the shade.

Dorahy was weeping hopelessly, the tears and the sweat griming his fanatic face. Let me back in there, he kept begging over and over, pushing beyond the constable's barrier arm at the closed courthouse door. Let me back.

Sorry, sir, said the constable, who was firm and kind as well. If you don't stop it, I'll have to take you in charge. He steered him to a bench alongside the hall. Just sit there, like, for a bit, he said. It's the bloody heat getting at us. That's what it is.

He stepped back and took up a guard's stance by the doorway.

Dorahy came to his senses slowly. He wiped his face off with the arm of his sleeve and sat there till the heart quietened. From the courthouse came the shuffling sounds of the assembly rising, but he didn't move. He sat his shame stubbornly there and watched as they came out, watched and watched and found no words for it.

I T IS the last night.

Take time over this, over the pathos engendered by the lamps, the slow rain on the iron roof of the hall, the wistfulness of streamers coming loose. There are too many people and by now some of them have lost the crack-hearty jauntiness of that first evening and have their faces settled into the lines that betray their age and a grief for it which they attribute to this last act of farewell.

They are wrong. They have simply regained themselves as they are, not as they used to be. They are simply a crowd of elderly people, disappointed by time, who are longing to get home. And this common denominator, home, is not what they have come to visit after all but that which they have left.

They are more critical of the place, too. Its shortcomings are beginning to be listed on their tongues. They know they could never settle here again. They are glad they got away. They are disappointed in each other: the fabled jokester, the hero of other years, is disguised by fat and wrinkles, is a feeble punster at that, who worries about his audience more than his words, is become a bore with ill-polished shoes and a suit that sags. The beauties have turned shrewish. God bless the lot of them, for the unpleasantnesses that once irritated are beginning to reassert themselves. Skins are peeled from eyes.

Barney Sweetman is chairing again. Buckmaster is by his side. Their wives are on stage as well, dried-out ladies who are over-powered by Gracie Tilburn, guest artist in lavender silk. The flowers in vases are all lies, and they are limp from strategy. The bunting is conscious of hypocrisy.

In this hall, noisy with conversation, last-minute recognitions and

128

bogus promises to keep in touch are made. It is sizzling with an amity in the centre of which Boyd's party is seated halfway from the door. Dorahy, pale with anticipation, can barely speak. Boyd, stocky as a bull, has his intransigent jaw set and jutting. He has the manic fanaticism of the recently converted.

When Sweetman stands and raises his hand for silence, the buzzing roar of the hall subsides as eyes focus on the big fellow who is more or less king of the kids, of the town, an infallible potentate. Up there he is speaking *ex cathedra,* and they prepare to hang on his lips.

"Dear old friends," he begins and his audience, strangely enough, instead of melting, hardens. They are not aware of it themselves, but they have fought forward to a sort of self-truth which sees themselves as less than friends. There have been too many petty arguments, too many misplaced remarks, a lack of delicacy in reminiscence; too much has been forgotten and too much remembered. "You are probably feeling tonight as I feel, tremendously sad on looking about this room and seeing faces familiar and meaning so much."

The crowd generously goes with him. After all it's a bugger of a job, this speech-making. But they go only a little way.

"We have had a week of recollections and memories, but more than that we have had a resurgence of the spirit—yes, the very spirit—that helped create this town. I find this moving, indeed." He pauses—it is a moment when he could have wiped his eyes but doubts the wisdom of the gesture coming too early. He goes on in a voice calculated to wring.

"The soul, or rather the life-blood of this town is its people. Yes. I say it again—those people who gave all they had to the building of it." A more weak-minded claque cheers. Some women dab hankies. "All we have built here," Sweetman continues, seizing the moment by its straggly forelock, "comes more or less from nothing. What you see now is the result of our work, our work and all we put into making this town what it is. I could name those people who are sitting before me with us tonight. But that would mean naming every one of you"—That's clever!—"and looking around at one another as you are now you see there, in the faces on each side of you, in front and behind, those who were the builders of the future."

Dorahy thinks he might vomit.

"In those days," Sweetman says, "you might remember the struggles we had with the south. You might recall the Separation League. The struggles to get coloured labour. The opposition from those who understood little and felt less about those problems peculiar to this part of the world. And all the time—I repeat, all the time—in the face of these difficulties, we pushed ahead doing what we believed to be right, sacrificing all for the sake of those who would come after."

Prolonged cheers. They are melting again.

"Yes," he continues when the blast subsides, "we were unpopular boys in the Separation League." He allows himself a roguish grin, but it comes out crooked. "We were firebrands then. Younger, of course. But firebrands. And I choose that word especially because we were burning with zeal to promote the interests of this town."

His choice of word stuns Boyd and Dorahy. The monstrous cheek of it, and Sweetman, legs apart, braced before his world!

"We were interested only in what concerned the good of us all. Dear friends, tonight, as you are on the eve of departure, I want you to take away memories of those times and remember how we fought together. No battle against the nation's enemies has more sincerity and strength than the battles we fought. There is no greater comradeship than that which we had." He stops to allow them all to dry their eyes. "Now that we are all of us nearing the twilight of our years, there is this we can remember—what I have said tonight will shine as youngly for you now as it did then."

The applause is sickeningly tremendous. People can drown in shallows. Dorahy is coughing into his wet hands while Sweetman smiles like a Messiah.

"And now," he says, "once again I have pleasure in asking your own Miss Gracie Tilburn to sing for you—as she sang earlier in the week—directly to your hearts."

There is another storm of clapping and the pianist comes on stage to the worn upright. Gracie, splendid in that fluid silk, moves to the front of the rostrum, inwardly hesitant despite that outer assurance, and Dorahy and Boyd hold their breaths. She is torn between what she has been asked to do and what the crowd expects—and it is a wink that does it.

Centre front, Freddie Buckmaster catches her eye and closes one of his in a huge and vulgar implication. Her disgust rejects him afresh, and she hears her own voice saying firmly and richly through the pianist's opening chords, "Ladies and gentlemen, before I sing to you

130

tonight, I ask you to give up a few minutes of your time to listen to Mr William Boyd. He has something to say to you all."

The audience is rattled. The pianist half turns. Sweetman, who has regained his seat in showers of light, starts up, but not before he sees in the heart of the hall Snoggers Boyd standing on his chair and circling so that he takes the entire gathering into his compelling eye.

There is some uncertain clapping and a lot of murmuring. As Gracie resumes her seat, an isolated cry of "Shame!" rings out.

Boyd is standing perched there above the goggling crowd, an un-impressive man except for his voice, which will have profound and resonant convictions. Carefully he waits until the silence of speculation has deepened and then he begins, speaking quietly.

"Ladies and gentlemen, I will not take up much of your time." He knows there isn't much. From the corner of his eye he can see Buck-master père on stage gesturing to his son. "As you know I have been writing a series of articles for you each day on the very people who have loomed large in the progress of this town." The silence has a trembling quality. The air quivers. "You are all aware," Boyd contin-ues, "of the misadventure that overtook the *Gazette* last Wednesday evening, when not only the next day's issue was destroyed but also the plates to set it up. When Mr Sweetman chose to speak of firebrands he couldn't have chosen a more apposite word, for the firebrands are still with us."

He lets his allegation rest in half a minute's tension. The hall rustles. They get it. There are shouts of "Sit down, old man!" from the Buckmaster claque, and Barney Sweetman is observed leaving the stage. But Boyd merely pitches his voice above the beginning din.

"My offices were destroyed, there is no doubt about this, deliber-ately"—he emphasises the word—"and perhaps by the very spirit which Mr Sweetman said animated some of us in past years. Who would do this, I do not know for certain. But I do suspect. What I do know is that I was going to tell you all of a humbler soul than those who waged battle in the Separation League, a humbler spirit than those who fought to use coloured labour cheap, a meeker spirit than those who waged unceasing war against the blacks. I am referring to Charles Lunt who is with us in the hall this evening."

The stillness is fragile. Boyd's wandering eye observes Sweetman in consultation with two bruisers of young men by the rear door.

"Perhaps," he goes on more loudly and strongly, "many of you did not know him. He was not a pushing man. It's more than likely you were unaware of him, for he practised his charity without airing it. But tragedy attended him. In his efforts to befriend those blacks who camped near his lonely farm, in his efforts to protect them, he lost a limb and almost lost his life."

On stage Buckmaster is going mad. His insanity boils blood, thickens features, clogs the shouts and gabbled directions he is trying to give his bully boys who have come up the aisle and are struggling to haul Boyd from his chair. As Boyd wobbles with the dragging arms, and as Lunt is seen to rise beside him stumped by his wooden leg, other shouts of "Fair go!" and "Give him a go!" rattle from all over the room. The audience has been split in half.

Gracie Tilburn, her red hair ablaze, rushes to the very footlights and pleads for silence. It is so outrageous for a woman to assert herself among men, the hall is temporarily shocked and muted. Fred Buckmaster, shoving his way along the side to get at Boyd, is so appalled he stops to screech at her, "Sit down you crazy bitch!" Some devotee clips his mouth for that, and another tussle starts.

Finally it is Barney Sweetman who shows reason. Politically. His angel face torn, his age humped all over his thinning shoulders, he cries high-pitchedly from the very back of the hall, "Stop this, everyone. Stop spoiling the week." His voice cracks suddenly with the effort of it. "Stop negating," he croaks, "those very qualities I spoke of. Stop!"

The crowd looks from Boyd to Sweetman, who cannily takes a punt on reasonableness. Shrewdly he guesses at the course the crowd, this mindless animal, will take. Boyd is a village innocent after all. Sweetman knows all about crowds.

"Let Boyd be heard," he pleads, giving his failed-playboy smile. He'll go down as a fair player if nothing else. "Everyone has a right to be heard."

The factions subside into murmurous dissidence while Boyd, flinging off the restraining arms, regains his balance. He gazes all about him and senses the split.

"As I was saying," he continues, "there was a certain night that year, twenty years ago, when Charles Lunt paid dearly for what he believed, when he paid for the very respect he gave humanity." Boyd goes on speaking more quietly and persuasively now. The awakened crowd, scandal-hungry, ravenously wants every word. ". . . and it was there that someone from the town, Tom Dorahy, in fact, found him, lashed to the dead body of his native friend." Boyd pauses and looks about the hall, but his eyes finally come to rest on the stage. Who would do a thing like this?" he asks. The crowd is stirring and whispering, but the whispers hiss. "And two days after this, as many of you remember, a trumped up vigilante force rode out to Mandarana and in cold blood dispatched six of the natives from Lunt's tribe. I call it Lunt's tribe, for they were dear to him. But more—one of the terrified gins flung herself over The Leap, her baby in her arms." The crowd is dumb with it. "It lived, that baby," Boyd says into the expecting silence. "It was cared for by my wife and me and then by the Jenners. You all remember her. And then, somehow, whether it was an instinctive turn towards the protector of her people we will never know, but that young woman sought out Charles Lunt and has cared for him these last few years."

Everywhere there are eyes, Boyd observes, polished and gleaming. They are watching his mouth, clutching at what it has to spill.

He says, "That was the story I intended telling you. It is nothing worth burning a building down for, as you can see, but it is worth the telling for it is simply another sample such as Mr Sweetman gave you of the martyrdoms this town exacted. Why anyone should want the story not told, you and I can only guess. It is a matter I leave to the consciences of those who tried to stop me. I make no accusations. The matter can stand there—but at least I have spoken out."

Sweetman has guessed aright.

The crowd is embarrassed now. It has been told things it did not wish to hear—not now, not when it has been softened into a spurious amity once again. The champion of their mediocrity is twitching on stage before their astounded eyes, and even their mediocrity by this turn of events has been belittled. Sweetman had given them an image of themselves to treasure, and now it has been scrawled upon by this other man. Some resent, even hate him for it. Others, believing in the imperial order of things, have their loyalties to the town powers cemented. And many, teased by Boyd's story, are filled with a grieving quality of love. Arguing and shouting break out. The crowd is two-headed. Everywhere people are standing and pushing out from their seats in an animal perplexity, and it is in vain that Sweetman shrills for order over the chaos.

As Boyd resumes his seat, the tension leaving him, he is suddenly aware of Lunt's face, an aged and dreadful white, bending towards him.

"Damn you," he is saying softly and penetratingly. "Damn you both. Damn you, damn you!"

He struggles upright, his wooden leg catching for a moment on that of a chair, and then he has shoved past the two of them to the aisle and is wrestling his way out through the crowd.

Shocked but immediately aware, Boyd is on his feet after him in silent pleading for understanding. Dorahy, stunned by this condemnation that has rammed the truth home at last, sits on for a few seconds, then, driven by an ego-wild need for absolution, fights his way up the aisle after them.

Through the sweet and the sour of it Lunt, Boyd and Dorahy push their way to the rear door. There is an acrid taste in the mouth. Arms seek to restrain them, either through love or hate. Hands clutch. Voices hail or accuse. But they can only shove sweatily through the praise and the blame towards the cooler rational night outside.

Buckmaster towering, blood-pressure up, is now screaming hoarsely for silence in the stifling room. He signals to the pianist and while she hits some expectant chords and while the audience, grudgingly accepting this signal at last, fights its way back to seats, the three squeezing through the doorway are conscious of having taken most of the hatred with them. And it is when they reach the top of the steps that some unknown, sour with self-disillusion, lurches out from the shadowed avengers who have been waiting for them and hurls Lunt brutally down the stairs.

From on stage Gracie Tilburn watches with horror, even as she takes up her position beside the piano, a small hate-pack headed by young Buckmaster, Romney and Armitage, surge out the double doors after them. She sees the Jenners jostled carelessly to one side; she glimpses Lunt being hurled and sees Boyd and Dorahy taking themselves after him.

Mechanically, she starts to sing.

Outside, Lunt is lying on the ground, his wooden leg hideously askew, his body sprawled face down. In his forced descent he has whacked his skull against a corner post and lies there utterly still. There is a small trickle of blood already blurred by rain.

Boyd bends over him, and then looks up at Dorahy.

134

"Well," he says bitterly, "you've had your martyr."

Then the pack is upon them, silent, and deadly because of this. The two men find themselves hauled by enemies who seem all clenched fist and boot to the private darknesses at the side of the hall where the gristle of their argument is stretched and torn.

While they endure the splitting punches and the duller agony of kicks, from inside the hall Gracie's voice rises liquidly in song. She is telling of old acquaintance as Dorahy goes down at last, seeing Boyd, his face dark with blood, leaning sideways in slow motion. Dorahy is so tired he accepts the fleshly damage of his enemies like some peculiar blessing, lying on the rain-wet grass, his lips curled in the smile of pain. Somewhere close beside him Boyd is groaning into the air as Gracie's voice soars and falls in nostalgic untruth.

The hate-pack is gone now, leaving them alone in the dark with the singing voice going on and on, endlessly it seems, through their battered ears. Full-throatedly, the audience joins in the singing and roars chorus after chorus.

It has almost forgotten the victims already.

# FOR THE BEST IN PAPERBACKS, LOOK FOR THE

In every corner of the world, on every subject under the sun, Penguin represents quality and variety—the very best in publishing today.

For complete information about books available from Penguin—including Pelicans, Puffins, Peregrines, and Penguin Classics—and how to order them, write to us at the appropriate address below. Please note that for copyright reasons the selection of books varies from country to country.

**In the United Kingdom:** For a complete list of books available from Penguin in the U.K., please write to *Dept E.P., Penguin Books Ltd, Harmondsworth, Middlesex, UB7 0DA.*

**In the United States:** For a complete list of books available from Penguin in the U.S., please write to *Dept BA, Penguin,* Box 120, Bergenfield, New Jersey 07621-0120.

**In Canada:** For a complete list of books available from Penguin in Canada, please write to *Penguin Books Ltd, 2801 John Street, Markham, Ontario L3R 1B4.*

**In Australia:** For a complete list of books available from Penguin in Australia, please write to the *Marketing Department, Penguin Books Ltd, P.O. Box 257, Ringwood, Victoria 3134.*

**In New Zealand:** For a complete list of books available from Penguin in New Zealand, please write to the *Marketing Department, Penguin Books (NZ) Ltd, Private Bag, Takapuna, Auckland 9.*

**In India:** For a complete list of books available from Penguin, please write to *Penguin Overseas Ltd, 706 Eros Apartments, 56 Nehru Place, New Delhi, 110019.*

**In Holland:** For a complete list of books available from Penguin in Holland, please write to *Penguin Books Nederland B.V., Postbus 195, NL-1380AD Weesp, Netherlands.*

**In Germany:** For a complete list of books available from Penguin, please write to *Penguin Books Ltd, Friedrichstrasse 10-12, D-6000 Frankfurt Main 1, Federal Republic of Germany.*

**In Spain:** For a complete list of books available from Penguin in Spain, please write to *Longman, Penguin España, Calle San Nicolas 15, E-28013 Madrid, Spain.*

**In Japan:** For a complete list of books available from Penguin in Japan, please write to *Longman Penguin Japan Co Ltd, Yamaguchi Building, 2-12-9 Kanda Jimbocho, Chiyoda-Ku, Tokyo 101, Japan.*

# FOR THE BEST IN PAPERBACKS, LOOK FOR THE

*Also available from King Penguin:*

☐ **THE DEPTFORD TRILOGY**
*Robertson Davies*

A glittering, fantastical, cunningly contrived trilogy of novels that centers on the mystery "Who killed Boy Staunton?," *Fifth Business, The Manticore,* and *World of Wonders* lure the reader through a labyrinth of myth, history, and magic.

"[Davies] conveys a sense of real life lived in a fully imagined . . . world."
— *New York Times Book Review*

864 pages       ISBN: 0-14-006500-8       **$8.95**

☐ **THE MONKEY'S WRENCH**
*Primo Levi*

Through the mesmerizing tales told by two characters—one, a construction worker/philosopher who has built towers and bridges in India and Alaska; the other, a writer/chemist, rigger of words and molecules—Primo Levi celebrates the joys of work and the art of storytelling.

"A further extension of Levi's remarkable sensibility, his survivor's sense of will . . . and his sense of humor" — *Washington Post Book World*

174 pages       ISBN: 0-14-010357-0       **$6.95**

☐ **THE PROGRESS OF LOVE**
*Alice Munro*

Hailed by *The New York Times Book Review* as "one of the best books of 1986," these eleven short stories feature characters who struggle in a brutal yet mysteriously beautiful world, telling us much about ourselves, our choices, and our experiences of love.

"Alice Munro is a born teller of tales." — *The Washington Post*

310 pages       ISBN: 0-14-010553-0       **$6.95**

You can find all these books at your local bookstore, or use this handy coupon for ordering:

**Penguin Books By Mail**
Dept. BA  Box 999
Bergenfield, NJ 07621-0999

Please send me the above title(s). I am enclosing _____
(please add sales tax if appropriate and $1.50 to cover postage and handling). Send check or money order—no CODs. Please allow four weeks for shipping. We cannot ship to post office boxes or addresses outside the USA. *Prices subject to change without notice.*

Ms./Mrs./Mr. _____

Address _____

City/State _____ Zip _____

**Sales tax:**  CA: 6.5%   NY: 8.25%   NJ: 6%   PA: 6%   TN: 5.5%

# FOR THE BEST IN PAPERBACKS, LOOK FOR THE

☐ **THE ELIZABETH STORIES**
*Isabel Huggan*

Smart, stubborn, shy, and giving, Elizabeth discovers all the miseries, and some of the wonders, of childhood. These delightful stories, showing her steely determination throughout a series of disasters and misunderstandings, remind us that if growing up is hard, it can also be hilarious.

"Twists and rings in the mind like a particularly satisfying and disruptive novel"
— *The New York Times Book Review*

    *184 pages*    *ISBN: 0-14-010199-3*    **$6.95**

☐ **FOE**
*J. M. Coetzee*

In this brilliant reshaping of Defoe's classic tale of Robinson Crusoe and his mute slave Friday, J. M. Coetzee explores the relationships between speech and silence, master and slave, sanity and madness.

"Marvelous intricacy and almost overwhelming power . . . *Foe* is a small miracle of a book." — *Washington Post Book World*

    *158 pages*    *ISBN: 0-14-009623-X*    **$6.95**

☐ **1982 JANINE**
*Alasdair Gray*

Set inside the head of an aging, divorced, insomniac supervisor of security installations who hits the bottle in the bedroom of a small Scottish hotel, *1982 Janine* is a sadomasochistic, fetishistic fantasy.

"*1982 Janine* has a verbal energy, an intensity of vision that has mostly been missing from the English novel since D. H. Lawrence."
— *The New York Times*

    *346 pages*    *ISBN: 0-14-007110-5*    **$6.95**

☐ **THE BAY OF NOON**
*Shirley Hazzard*

An Englishwoman working in Naples, young Jenny has no friends, only a letter of introduction—a letter that leads her to a beautiful writer, a famous Roman film director, a Scottish marine biologist, and ultimately to a new life.

"Drawn so perfectly that it seems to breathe"
— *The New York Times Book Review*

    *154 pages*    *ISBN: 0-14-010450-X*    **$6.95**

☐ **THE WELL**
*Elizabeth Jolley*

Against the stark beauty of the Australian farmlands, Elizabeth Jolley paints the portrait of an eccentric, affectionate relationship between two women—Hester, a lonely spinster, and Katherine, a young orphan. Their simple, satisfyingly pleasant life is nearly perfect until a dark stranger invades their world in a most horrifying way.

"An exquisite story . . . Jolley [has] a wonderful ear, [and] an elegant and compassionate voice." — *The New York Times Book Review*

    *176 pages*    *ISBN: 0-14-008901-2*    **$6.95**

# FOR THE BEST IN PAPERBACKS, LOOK FOR THE

☐ **GOD'S SNAKE**
*Irini Spanidou*

Irini Spanidou's debut novel is the remarkable, timeless tale of Anna, the daughter of a proud and brutal army officer and his disillusioned wife, who struggles to grow up in the ravaged landscape of post-War Greece.

"Remarkably fresh and vigorous . . . An impressive achievement"
— *The New York Times Book Review*

252 pages · ISBN: 0-14-010360-0 **$6.95**

☐ **THE LAST SONG OF MANUEL SENDERO**
*Ariel Dorfman*

In an unnamed country, in a time that might be now, the son of Manuel Sendero refuses to be born, beginning a revolution where generations of the future wait for a world without victims or oppressors.

"A profound lament for humanity's lost innocence, a chronicle of despair, and a fervent hymn of hope" — *San Francisco Chronicle*

464 pages ISBN: 0-14-008896-2 **$7.95**

☐ **THE CHILD IN TIME**
*Ian McEwan*

When his three-year-old daughter is kidnapped from his side, Stephen Lewis drinks too much and dreams of her—both as she was and as he imagines she has become. Like his daughter, he too is lost in time, as past, present, and future meld.

"Beautifully constructed and brilliantly sustained . . . *The Child in Time* is born a near masterpiece." — *San Francisco Chronicle*

264 pages ISBN: 0-14-011246-4 **$7.95**

---

You can find all these books at your local bookstore, or use this handy coupon for ordering:

**Penguin Books By Mail**
Dept. BA Box 999
Bergenfield, NJ 07621-0999

Please send me the above title(s). I am enclosing _____
(please add sales tax if appropriate and $1.50 to cover postage and handling). Send check or money order—no CODs. Please allow four weeks for shipping. We cannot ship to post office boxes or addresses outside the USA. *Prices subject to change without notice.*

Ms./Mrs./Mr. _____

Address _____

City/State _____ Zip _____

**Sales tax:**   CA: 6.5%   NY: 8.25%   NJ: 6%   PA: 6%   TN: 5.5%

## FOR THE BEST IN PAPERBACKS, LOOK FOR THE

☐ **THE NEWS FROM IRELAND**
  *William Trevor*

This major collection of short stories once again shows Trevor's extraordinary power. In the title story, his evocation of the anguished relations of an Anglo-Irish family through several generations approaches the dramatic and forceful effect of a full novel.

"Trevor is perhaps the finest short story writer in the English language." — *Vanity Fair*                                286 pages       ISBN: 0-14-008857-1       **$6.95**

☐ **THE SHRAPNEL ACADEMY**
  *Fay Weldon*

At a military school named for the inventor of the exploding cannonball, perhaps it should come as no surprise when the annual Eve-of-Waterloo dinner, for which the guest list includes a young weapons salesman and a reporter for a feminist newspaper, hilariously and spontaneously combusts.

"This is Fay Weldon's funniest novel . . . an original, unconventional comedy." — *San Francisco Chronicle*
                        186 pages       ISBN: 0-14-009746-5       **$6.95**

☐ **SAINTS AND STRANGERS**
  *Angela Carter*

In eight dazzling, spellbinding stories, Angela Carter draws on familiar themes and tales—Peter and the Wolf, Lizzie Borden, *A Midsummer Night's Dream*—and transforms them into enchanting, sophisticated, and often erotic reading for modern adults.

"Whimsical, mischievous, and able to work magic . . . Carter's stories disorient and delight." — *Philadelphia Inquirer*
                        126 pages       ISBN: 0-14-008973-X       **$5.95**

☐ **IN THE SKIN OF A LION**
  *Michael Ondaatje*

Through intensely visual images and surreal, dreamlike episodes, Michael Ondaatje spins a powerful tale of fabulous adventure and exquisite sensuality set against the bridges, waterways, and tunnels of 1920s Toronto.

"A brilliantly imaginative blend of history, lore, passion, and poetry" — Russell Banks                        244 pages       ISBN: 0-14-011309-6       **$7.95**

☐ **THE GUIDE: A NOVEL**
  *R. K. Narayan*

Raju was once India's most corrupt tourist guide; now, after a peasant mistakes him for a holy man, he gradually begins to play the part. He succeeds so well that God himself intervenes to put Raju's new holiness to the test.

"A brilliant accomplishment" — *The New York Times Book Review*
                        220 pages       ISBN: 0-14-009657-4       **$5.95**